Gen X Praise* for
GUINEVERE MACKENZIE IS NOT A NICE GIRL

"This book is basically a time machine to 1981, minus the nuclear attack drills. It felt like I was sitting in front of the boob tube, eating dry cereal from the box, and praying the antenna would work long enough to watch *Facts of Life*."

> *- Cynthia,*
> *just a sniff of scented lip gloss brings it all back*

"Finally, a book that not only remembers we existed, but gets it right: the latchkey afternoons, distrust of authority, and belief that microwaves were peak tech."

> *- Jason,*
> can't let go of his Commodore 64 and that stack of floppy discs

"Highly recommend but be warned: it may cause you to dig out an old yearbook, or cry quietly to the old mixtape you hid in the underwear drawer."

> *- Tammy,*
> still keeps a box of notes from high school folded into complicated triangles

*as imagined by the author

Also by Jennifer Sneed

A Story Unwritten

Guinevere MacKenzie is NOT a *Nice Girl*

*How one girl endured her
weirdo parents, Freshman Year, and 1981…
and lived to tell the tale.*

Jennifer Sneed

OONA ISLE
BOOKS
TULSA, OK

Cover Design: Karina Granda

Publisher's Cataloging-in-Publication Data

Names: Sneed, Jennifer, author.

Title: Guinevere MacKenzie is not a nice girl : how one girl endured her weirdo parents , freshman year, and 1981...and lived to tell the tale / Jennifer Sneed.

Description: Tulsa, OK: Oona Isle Books, 2025.

Identifiers: LCCN: 2025910054 | ISBN: 979-8-9909414-5-8 (hardcover) | 979-8-9909414-4-1 (paperback) | 979-8-9909414-6-5 (ebook) | 979-8-9909414-7-2 (audio)

Subjects: LCSH High school--Fiction. | Friendship--Fiction. | Cheerleading--Fiction. | Generation X—Fiction. | Oklahoma--Fiction. | Christian life--Fiction. | Nineteen eighties--Fiction. | Coming of age--Fiction. | Bildungsroman. | Historical fiction. | BISAC FICTION / Coming of Age | FICTION / Historical / 20th Century / General | FICTION / Humorous / General

Classification: LCC PS3619. N44 G85 2025 | DDC 813.6--dc23

To my grandparents:

Wanda and Jerry,

Cora and Robert,

Forrest Wayne and Myra.

For thinking I was extraordinary, despite evidence to the

contrary.

Time present and time past
Are both perhaps present in time future,
And time future contained in time past.
T.S. Eliot

Chapter 1
Time is Time

Six middle-aged women walk into a hotel bar.

The formula requires a punchline, but these women won't provide it unless they can write it themselves and stand on the bar to deliver it, tip jar at their feet.

No complaints will be lodged with the manager. No unreasonable demands will be made to the waitstaff, though the muscle-bound blonde will certainly endure some gentle flirtation. These women are not dead yet. And because they haven't forgotten where they came from, their gratuity will be generous.

These friends—my friends—are upstanding enough to be respectable, but not too much to have fun.

We haven't seen each other in years, though we do keep up. It's a multiple-of-ten reunion weekend, and we're beginning the celebration early at a lakeside resort. Conversation is polite as we test the waters of our old friendship.

"How are you?"

"The kids?"

"The grandkids?"

"The blood pressure?"

"The husband?"

"Retired?!"

"How nice."

"Wish mine was."

Bottles of wine are opened at a table overlooking the marina.

"I gave up wine for Lent."

"It's June, Lent is over."

"Well, in that case…"

The hunky waiter heavily pours the red and the white. "What are you ladies celebrating?"

"That we didn't marry our high school crush."

"Except this one." They point and glasses are raised.

"Some people have all the luck."

After the first glass, polite walls crumble, honesty breaks free.

"Middle-aged? Is that what we're calling ourselves?"

"Only if we live to 114."

"The blood pressure is terrible. I shouldn't be drinking this but give me another. One more. It's good to be here. Away from it all."

Two glasses in, the stories turn to menopause and poor decisions. Who said and did what to whom. Of people unknown to me but interesting just the same. Tales told with pinkened cheeks in a rush of inhibition unlikely to be regretted later. These are friends, good friends. We keep secrets.

And so, blood pressure be damned, I ask for another bottle for the table. My treat, I sold a story. But not that bottle. The house white, please. It was a small story, an unknown magazine, a pittance really. Economies must be kept; he retired, you know.

Laughter abounds.

After the third glass, conversation slows. Flush with the warmth of wine and good company, thoughts turn inward. How did I end up here, in this place, with these friends, and this full life?

The conversation turns.

"Do you remember?"

"Remember the time..."

"Remember when our biggest worry was..."

"When I was twelve...

thirteen...

fourteen."

Remember. Remember. Remember.

The breeze lifting off the sun-soaked, moon-dappled water wafts past my cheek, and I cast my line into the lake of memory, grown murky from mud stirred up as I wade through it. I pull out a whopper: the spring I turned fourteen, was sick to death of being weird, heard a call from the Lord, and decided to change my fate.

I gaze past my old friends at the sky, speckled with starlight, and I remember how I got here, how it started. I see it all.

The street.

The house.

The porch.

The girl. Waiting. Suitcase beside her.

With dusk closing in.

Chapter 2
Spring 1981

"Guinevere, come inside before you're eaten alive. He's not coming."

Mom slammed the screen door, its resounding bang laden with exasperation at my father. He hadn't called to say he wasn't coming, but as he was two hours late, it was strongly implied. The slam's echo rebounded her frustration to me for being mule-headed enough to sit on the front step, clutching my small suitcase for two whole hours while I waited.

"He's coming!" My shout reverberated through the lowering dusk, disturbing the cloud of mosquitoes hovering over my head, ready to dive in for a snack. They weren't deterred for long, though. Fair and freckled, I glowed under the porchlight, a beacon for every biting insect for miles around. Mamaw said fair and freckled was the favorite treat of the Okie skeeter, and I hadn't seen evidence to contradict her. I slapped a plump one feasting on my kneecap. Its guts gushed.

"He's not coming," I whispered to the gross splotch, finally admitting the sad truth: I'd been forgotten again.

Geesh, why couldn't I be normal? A tanned Stacy with straight teeth and hair that didn't frizz at the slightest provocation. A girl with normal parents who didn't, under any circumstances, name their progeny a romance-tinged, hippie-inspired name like Guinevere. A girl whose father showed up on his weekend.

I slumped into the house, kicking aside a tuna fish can that one of the cats had been playing with. Mom stared me down, one hand on her extra-curvy hip. Her eyelids were coated in the smoky eyeshadow design she'd copied from Cosmo, page sixty-seven, "Eyes to Make the Men Go Wild." I knew because I read her magazines when she wasn't looking.

"I had plans, Guinevere. A well-deserved and needed night out. And now I'm forced to stay home."

"How is it my fault? I can go to Mamaw's if you want."

"Tonight's her square dance group, I already checked."

"At least somebody's having fun."

Her look said she was above my sarcasm and would not stoop to acknowledge it.

"Why don't you go out and leave me here?"

She raised her eyebrow.

"I'm fourteen!"

"Barely."

"So? Fourteen and one month is still fourteen."

"You don't act like it. Last time you stayed home alone, you left a pot of mac and cheese on the stove and almost burned the house down."

"For the millionth time, I'm sorry. It was an accident."

"Never have been able to get that pot clean."

I rolled my eyes. If I apologized a trillion times, she'd still never forgive me.

"Eye rolling? Seriously?"

She walked away muttering about unfairness, cross-bearing, and my lousy, no-good father.

I retreated to my room, closed the door, and breathed in the calming scent of Lemon Pledge. My bedroom was my sanctuary, a place of order in the litter-strewn chaos of my drab existence.

Taking care not to mess up the artful arrangement of pillows I'd labored over that morning, I collapsed back on my bed and stared at the poster collage of Scott Baio on the wall.

"Why's life so unfair, Scott?"

He didn't answer. I flipped over on my belly and opened *These Happy Golden Years.* I'd read it a thousand times, along with all the other Little House books, but it was still my favorite because of the romance. I was re-reading the part where Almonzo proposes, when the familiar smell of Charlie, Mom's favorite perfume, permeated the atmosphere.

She's changed her mind, I sighed, marking the page with my thumb.

She stood in the doorway, one hand on the doorknob. Two of her cats ran in around her feet.

"Out, out damn cats!" I jumped up and herded them right out the door, blocking the entrance with my body. My room was my pet-free paradise, my cat-hair-free zone.

"Mom! You're supposed to knock. Isn't privacy like a Constitutional right or something?"

She rolled her eyes. A clear case of do as I say and not as I do. "How did I spawn such a weird kid?"

"If I knew the answer to that question, my life would be a million times better.

She sighed heavily before flipping her hair. "I've changed my mind. I'm going out and you're coming with me. Change out of those gross cut-offs."

Before I could respond, she walked away. It was for the best because I had nothing nice to say.

Groaning and grumbling—and low-level swearing—I looked in my closet. I didn't know where we were going, but I could narrow it down to two possibilities: the head shop or the Jesus Freaks. Contrary to accepted logic, it was the same group at both places: delusional people who wanted to forget it was 1981 and their hippie days were over. Places where Mom talked to men who wrote poetry and were in touch with their feelings.

According to Mamaw, Mom only liked men who didn't know how to do anything and weren't going anywhere. I figured Mamaw should know because my step-Grandpa Gerald can fix anything, and they're going to Arizona on their next vacation.

Either way, stoners or holy-rollers, I was going to do my best to prove I didn't fit in with their general grodiness.

My favorite outfit was a red plaid jumper that I wore over a white blouse with puffed sleeves and a bow at the neck. I found it at a garage sale in one of the rich neighborhoods across the river where Mamaw liked to shop. She was a first-class garage saler and was teaching me the ropes.

The outfit looked like something Marcia Brady wore in a rerun of *The Brady Bunch*, a show I watched because Greg Brady was a total fox. Marcia's puffed sleeves had the advantage of setting me apart from Mom's shower-optional hippie friends because nothing says, "I'm totally ordinary" like the Bradys. To make myself super-duper ordinary, I spritzed Love's Baby Soft on my wrists.

"Leaving now!" Mom slammed the screen door.

I followed her outside to the embarrassing car in our driveway, a 1974 Ford Gran Torino, red with a white swoosh that began at the headlights and rushed along the side until it curved up and around the back seat window. The rising swoop held the promise of speed. The boldness of its sweep—rampant on the red field—swaggered. It stated with dumb confidence that it was a cool car for a cool person. A bold purchasing decision for those who won't take no for an answer.

It was a big, fat lie.

When *Starsky and Hutch* sped around town in an identical car, chasing criminals and fighting crime, it was cool, but those days had passed. The show was in reruns, and so was the car. And to make matters worse, the iconic style made it impossible to pretend it was anything but used—well-used, with the rattling muffler to prove it.

It was the bane of my banes.

The Swoosh Mobile.

With a grimace, I slid into the passenger seat, still not knowing where we were going, and squeezed my feet into the sliver of space not overtaken by the two-ton bag of cat food in the floorboard.

"Sorry. I forgot to take it in," Mom said.

"I can do it now," I offered. Not only would it give me more room, but it would also clear the air of the dusty tuna and salmon odor.

"No. Later. I'll do it later."

"Can we at least put it in the back? This thing's going to flatten my feet like pancakes the first time you turn a corner."

"Don't be melodramatic." She turned the key in the ignition, making the engine sputter, spurt, and cough. She smacked the dashboard. The engine hummed. "Besides, there's no room back there."

I looked over my shoulder; she wasn't wrong. The back seat was invisible, obscured by a jumble of nursing text-books, Styrofoam hamburger containers, a bag of cat litter big enough for every cat in the neighborhood, an elven cape, a shawl, a jaunty beret, and a decrepit birdcage she'd been meaning to drop off at Goodwill for about a month.

The gears grumbled as Swooshie refused to reverse. Mom smacked the dash again.

Before I knew it was happening, my thoughts tumbled out of my mouth, "You know, the car might work better if it wasn't being used as an 18-wheeler on a long haul."

"I don't need your snide remarks! This is my time. My night. You sound like my mother," she spat out. She followed up with indecipherable muttering, which I'm pretty sure was about my dad's failure to pick me up on his court-ordered weekend, and her regret at having a kid when she was only seventeen. Fourteen years later, and she was still going on about it.

"Then let me stay home."

She closed her smoky-eyeshadow-covered eyes and gave the dash a real wallop. And with a backward lurch, we were on our way.

I flipped on the radio and let me tell you, nothing could make Linda Ronstadt sound bad, not the tension in the car, not the rattling birdcage in the back seat, and not the staticky reception we got because the radio antenna got broken off by the previous car owners, probably in a high-speed pursuit gone wrong.

I sang along to take my mind off the three-ton bag of cat food that fell on my feet when we pulled onto the expressway. As we crossed the sand-bar-strewn Arkansas River, heading to the civilized side of the city where the air was free from the smell of the refinery, I crooned along to "Hurt So Bad" in a nasal voice. Nasal because I held my nose to block out the noxious bouquet of chemicals spewing from the refinery.

"Don't sing that," Mom snapped, "it's inappropriate."

"Why? Is it about sex or something?"

Her lips formed a prim line, leading me to believe our destination was the Jesus Inn. And when we exited the freeway just after we crossed the river, I knew it. I didn't understand why she was being prissy. A lot of the people who went to her church were recovering drug addicts. They had bigger problems than a sexy Linda Ronstadt song.

With a jerk and a cloud of toxic black smoke, we pulled into the parking lot of the strip mall where the church was located.

I petted the dashboard. "Poor Swooshie."

Some guys from the church ran out to help. It mainly amounted to praying over the car and laying hands on it, though one guy did pop the hood and stare at the engine. It was kind of nice, but I couldn't see it helping. I was guessing God had bigger things to worry about. Luckily, Grandpa Gerald had the skill to bring the Swoosh-mobile back from the brink of death.

None of the people surrounding the car noticed me. The Jesus Inn was strictly Mom's deal, like the cats were her cats. Her friends, her church of the moment, her out-let. She talked a big talk sometimes about wanting me to like the things she liked, but she got antsy when I did, like she was afraid I'd somehow take them away from her. I wandered away to let her have the spotlight.

The church used to be a store. Inside were a bunch of folding metal chairs, outlining an empty oval of linoleum where the pastor and band stood. I don't know why they bothered setting up so many chairs because it was a standing-up, swaying, and lifting-your-hands kind of church—the kind where people shouted *Groovy* along with their *Hallelujahs*. Sometimes, they even sat on the floor.

For a while, before he switched to being a Quaker, my dad was an Episcopalian. They had beautiful, padded pews, plus a padded bench that folded down, so your knees didn't get sore when you prayed. It was nice. Normal. Though—and I can't believe I'm saying this—maybe a little too normal. Truth be told, it was kind of boring.

The service at The Jesus Inn was a little like the Assembly of God church I went to with Mamaw sometimes, but the vibe was different.

Mom's church had a laundromat on one side and a nice steak restaurant on the other. The restaurant was expensive, so I'd never been there, but I had been to the laundromat to get a can of pop from the vending machine. My guess was that nobody at the Inn ate at the steak restaurant because some of them didn't wear shoes.

I grabbed a chair by the window and picked up a religious tract. It had comics, and there was nothing else to read. Besides, there was nothing—I repeat, nothing—more disturbing than watching your mom flirt, especially with the pervy pervs who looked at my chest when she wasn't looking.

Luckily, Mom's best friend showed up to run interference. Unluckily, she brought her son with her.

"Cherry!" Mom shouted.

"Fawn!"

They hugged each other, and the sleazeballs slunk away.

Mom and Cherry had been friends since elementary school. They were even pregnant at the same time, a story I'd heard again and again. That meant I'd known Cherry's son Timmy my whole life. He thought we were destined to get married one day, and the moms didn't do much to put him off the idea.

The best thing that had ever happened to me up to that point was when Cherry moved out to the boonies, which meant Timmy and I didn't go to the same school anymore. That earned a *Hallelujah* and a *Groovy* in my opinion. And when a thing like that is the best thing that's happened to you, it's a sure sign that your life stinks.

I hid behind the tract, but it was no good. It was one of those pocket-sized ones.

"What's up, Guinevere?"

"Hi, Timmy." I lowered the instructions for making Jesus my personal Lord and Savior. "How's it going?"

"Can't complain. It's almost summer."

"Three weeks. And we'll be Freshmen. Only four more years of school." I shook my head in disbelief. It was getting real, and I hadn't done anything yet except almost burn the house down.

"*Only* four years? That's a long prison sentence serving The Man." He hee-hawed and pulled up his tube socks.

I did not share his opinion. School was not a prison. It was a gateway to better things. And I was good at it. Conversation chilled. I couldn't believe this loser proposed marriage to me when we were five. I gave him my head tilted, eyes to the ceiling, look of disapproval.

"Don't have a cow, Guinevere. I just don't like school like you do. It sucks balls."

I reminded myself that he was Cherry's son, and I liked Cherry.

"Interesting opinion. Whatcha doing this summer?"

He groaned. "Going to summer school."

"Splendid."

"You?"

"I don't know. Hanging out at the park pool, I guess."

"Wish I could be there," he said with a catch in his breath.

He was looking at my chest instead of my face. I swear, I was the skinniest girl with the biggest boobs in existence. Mamaw said I'd always looked like a string bean, but when puberty hit, I looked like a string bean with tumors. Sometimes she even said it in front of people, which made me pray a hole would open in the floor and I'd fall into it.

"10-4, good buddy. My eyes are up here."

He blushed but tried to pass it off by brushing back his oily hair. "What's with the outfit? You look kind of stuck-up. Like Blair on *The Facts of Life*."

"Thank you."

Our stilted conversation ground to a halt. He wasn't sure if I was being sarcastic or not. Honestly, I wasn't sure either. I didn't want to be stuck-up, but being compared to Blair in a fashion sense was a first for me, and I liked it. And seriously, who was Timmy to comment on my fashion choices? I was positive he hadn't washed his lanky black hair in a week, maybe a month. And he'd definitely been storing his wrinkled Def Leppard t-shirt in a pile on the floor. We were incompatible; I liked Andy Gibb, and he liked Black Sabbath.

Besides, he was going nowhere. Fast. I'd read enough Cosmo to know that if I married him or someone like him, I'd spend my life living in a trailer park with a bong on every table. A cold sweat overcame me every time I thought about it. Could a girl from an off-the-wall family expect anything else? Anything more?

Luckily, the music started. Thank you, Jesus. And I meant it. At all the different churches I'd been to, singing was the best part. I rushed forward to join the congregation and left Timmy to talk to some other teens who had been dragged there by their parents.

Three acoustic guitars and a second-hand electronic piano joined together to make a beautiful sound. Dozens and dozens of grubby people, most of whom couldn't sing a toot, raised their voices, making a sound so glorious, you'd be forgiven for thinking they were angels. Even I, Guinevere MacKenzie, forgot I was a sarcastic, complaining grump who was confused about everything those days; an unsteady alto who changed chords whenever the urge struck me. When I joined the angel choir, I felt like an angel too.

In truth, the only one in the storefront church who would have sounded like an angel to outside ears was Mom. A dramatic soprano, her voice soared so high that you knew it would catch the attention of heaven to listen to our prayers.

Songs over, sermon beginning, I returned by hazy, rose-tinted routes to my chair by the window, warmed and comforted that God had a plan for me. A plan for more than a life with Timmy or someone like him. For more than the touch-and-go, just getting by life that my parents lived. A plan for good and not disaster. And boy, oh boy, did I need that because disaster followed me like a stomachache followed an extra-large, suicide slushie.

But how could I keep disaster at bay?

And just like that, I received a sign from heaven.

A brand new, pale gray, four-door Pontiac Bonneville parked in the lot in front of the steak restaurant. Understated, with no lying swoop, it was as long as a city block, with a trunk so wide you could get a 10-ton bag of cat food in there. A family got out. The dad wore a tie. His hair was short. The mom's hair swooped over her eyes like Farrah Fawcett's. She wore a skirt and sensible pumps like mothers do. Their daughter, about my age, wore a green and white cheerleading jacket with her name embroidered on the white flap hanging down the back: Libby.

Libby walked between her parents with her chin up. They would never embarrass her by dressing like an elf in public or wearing weird vests, which were not manly, no matter what Dad said. They talked together. Smiled. The dad stroked his daughter's dirty-blonde hair. My hair was the same color as Libby in her cheerleading jacket. I closed my eyes and ran my hand over my hair from crown to split ends, imagining a fatherly hand was doing it.

The family was orderly. Peaceful. As normal as normal could be.

Behind me, the music played, the people raised their hands, the pastor said, "Come you who are heavy laden..."

Boy was I laden. And was it ever heavy.

I was nothing like the girl out there, but if I were? If I were, maybe my dad would show up on his weekend. Maybe Mom wouldn't feel I was a cross to bear. Maybe Matt Madewell would ask me to go with him.

"...lay down your burdens, and I will give you rest."

It was the remedy to my messy, chaotic life. I knew God's plan for me, but I needed help achieving it.

I closed my eyes. I said the prayer. "Mighty God, please make me...normal."

But how? It was going to take a miracle.

I caught a final glimpse of the girl's cheerleading jacket as the family walked into the restaurant.

And like a bolt from Heaven, I knew what to do. I'd call Wendy Walters. Not only was she the most normal person who had ever set foot in West Junior High, but she needed help to pass eighth grade. I knew because after school, she'd tried to bribe me to do her work. I'd turned her down. But now? Praise God Almighty, did I have a deal for her.

Chapter 3

Give Me an O for Ordinary

EIGHTY PERCENT OF THE most embarrassing experiences of my life happened in gym class. It was therefore astonishing that I was standing in the recreation center's gymnasium on a Friday after school on a purely extracurricular basis.

The gym smelled like sweaty socks and overactive pituitary glands.

And I was seriously beginning to question my sanity. To question if I'd been called by God or only hepped up on praise songs. But in this case, The Call and my desires lined up perfectly, so I was sticking to the plan. Suffering through cheerleader tryouts would be worth it if I could join the ranks of the normal girls for once in my life. And where I lived, the normal girls were cheerleaders.

My old sneakers shed flakes of rubber as I traced the ear of the blue panther painted at center court. They were rapidly disintegrating thanks to a failed experiment with bleach. I had wanted my shoes to be shining white for the tryout so the judges would be so dazzled by my flashing feet that they'd miss my Herkie jump, which was still pathetic despite spending the last two weeks being tutored by Wendy in the fine art of cheerleading.

She told me if I messed up, I could make up points with my "show of spirit." I was hoping my cries of "Go, Panthers! Hold those Tigers!" would work in my favor, even though one of my rubber bands popped off my braces when I was yelling and came dangerously close to hitting one of the judges—none other than Mr. Randolph Bates Wilson.

Wendy stood to the left of me in the center of the cheerleader-since-birth group, the shining star in their galaxy. Each of them had real Keds sneakers on their feet, blue and white ribbons on their ponytails, and names ending in y: Tracy, Stacy, Becky, and Lori, which is not a y, but may as well be.

Orbiting this galaxy, waiting to be drawn in by its gravity, were lesser satellites with gleaming shoes and ribbons. They got the memo. One of them even had blue and white bands on her braces. Talk about commitment.

I ran a hand over my poor, bare ponytail. A cheerleading disgrace.

Wendy quietly raised her thumb to tell me it would be fine, but she didn't invite me to join the group. It was alright. I understood. I wasn't on the squad yet. And it was so nice of her to teach me cheerleading. In exchange, all I did was "help" her with the final book report of eighth grade, which was code for "I did it for her and put her name on it." It would be totally worth it when I made the squad, though. Wendy said everyone made it.

On my right was the only other person not included in Wendy's constellation: Charity Louise in her ankle-length culottes and turtleneck. She was serious about religion, so serious that I never would have suspected her as a closet cheerleader. But then again, most people would be surprised when they heard I'd made cheerleader. I wasn't exactly the cheerleader type, with my skinny, too-long legs the color of one of those blind cavefish.

Across from us, lined up on the black line underneath the basketball goal, were four empty metal chairs. Any minute, the judges would come back in, return to their seats, and announce my fate.

When the door swung open, the girls in Wendy's group broke their huddle and lined up. Wendy bounced on her toes and crossed her fingers like she was worried about making the squad. Everyone already knew she'd made it. One of the judges was her mom.

The chair squeaked when Mrs. Walters' bony butt skooched to find a comfortable position. As cheer sponsor and president of the PTA, the book drive, the bake sale, and the fall dance, she had her finger on the pulse of our little neighborhood on the wrong side of the Arkansas River.

The other judges included Nikki, the cheer coach who was on the Varsity squad at the high school. Wendy's cousin's sister said that Nikki was being recruited to be a Dallas Cowboys Cheerleader, and though I couldn't verify it, it seemed possible. Nikki could jump and touch both of her toes at the same time.

Then there was Mr. Roland. The metal chair groaned dangerously when he sat on it. Despite being the football coach, he looked like he'd never exercised a day in his life.

And finally, there was Mr. Randolph Bates Wilson, president of the booster club and owner of the Randolph Bates Wilson Insurance Agency, whose ads were painted on the fence around the football field. He waved at Lori.

"Hi, Daddy!" She waved back.

Lori would make the squad again.

Nikki clutched the paper bearing my fate. She cleared her throat and said in a voice trained to echo across the length and breadth of a football field, "Thanks for coming out today. Everyone did great, but remember, there are a limited number of spots on the squad. We'd like to welcome the following girls to Freshman Cheer. Lori Bates Wilson..."

"I can't believe it," Lori squealed.

I rolled my eyes.

"Wendy Walters..."

"I made it!" Wendy and her ponytail bounced.

I figured my name would be somewhere near the end. I settled in to wait. I'd had loads of practice waiting in gym class because I was always the last one picked for teams, even after Delmer Dinkins, and he weighed about a ton. The only thing I'd ever been picked first for was the spelling bee, and maybe a book report.

While Nikki announced names and a succession of girls squealed their surprise, I imagined what my response would be when my name was read.

"Who, me? I can't believe it." I'd clap my hands to my cheeks while sparkling tears appeared in the corner of my eyes.

"Welcome to the squad." The girls would gather around, ignoring my grody sneakers and lack of ribbons. "We always knew you were one of us."

The grinding squeak of metal chairs being folded and stacked brought me back to reality.

Wendy and her groupies were leaving the gym in one big, hugging, crying, "I can't believe I made it" group. The judges followed, averting their eyes from me and Charity Louise as we stood at center court.

It wasn't the first time daydreaming had caused me to miss my moment.

Charity Louise's eyes were closed when I looked over at her. I hated to interrupt her prayer, but I needed to know.

"Did they call? All the names?"

"Everyone's except mine and yours." She fingered the cross on her necklace.

"But Wendy said...There must be a mistake."

"Would you like to pray about it, Guinevere?"

"No. I'm good."

She looked disappointed. "Well, I'll be going then. Jesus bless you." With a backward wave, she walked toward the exit, culottes swishing around her ankles.

"Charity Louise," I called to her, "why did you try out? No offense, but it doesn't seem like your thing."

She paused with one hand on the door's push bar. Looking soulfully at me, she placed her other hand over her heart. "My pastor said we should get more involved in school so we can witness to our classmates."

"I see." And I did. I'd been around religion enough to know she was telling the truth.

"What about you? Do you have a personal relationship with the Lord Jesus Christ?"

"Believe me, we're lousy with the Lord at my house."

She didn't believe me; I could tell by the raised eyebrow.

"Why did you try out, Guinevere? It doesn't seem like your thing, either."

"Because cheerleading is the most normal thing a girl can do in 1981."

"No offense, but since when have you been worried about being normal?"

"Exactly."

With a shrug, she pressed the push bar. *Ka-thump.* "I'll pray for you." And she was gone.

I needed to talk to Coach Nikki to clear up this mistake, but outside, she was talking to the mothers, handing out packets about summer cheer camp and uniforms. I caught her eye, and she said in her cheery way, "Nice try. Maybe next time."

There was no mistake.

A few of the moms gave me a sympathetic look. The rest smirked. I suspected the smirking ones had noticed my mom's absence. I could imagine the conversation they'd have when I was out of earshot: "Guinevere MacKenzie's mom isn't here to pick her up. Guinevere Mackenzie's mom has never been to a PTA meeting. Guinevere MacKenzie isn't allowed to sell candy bars after the unfortunate incident in third grade. And her dad? Don't get me started. What a weirdo family."

Bitches!

I looked for Charity Louise, but she was getting into a Chevy Malibu station wagon. Blue. Brand new. I didn't feel bad for her with a nice car like that to ride home in.

The gaggle of cheerleaders exclaimed that they couldn't believe they made it to a group of high school boys.

Well-established. Get a new line. Cheerleaders are dumb.

But then Wendy bumped my shoulder with hers. "Guinie? What happened? Was it your splits?"

"More of a splat," I admitted.

"Herkie?"

"Spasmodic turkey."

"Oh, fudgsicles!"

"What the heck?" I burst out laughing. One of the things I'd learned while Wendy taught me is that she had the dirtiest mouth I'd ever heard, except for my Uncle Robin, who was an actual sailor. But then, I noticed Mrs. Walters frowning our way. No wonder Wendy was taking the name of a frozen treat in vain. Her mom would freak out if she heard half the stuff her daughter said. Wendy had obviously seen her mom looking. Smart girl.

"Oh, right, fudgsicles." I nodded.

"Come to my house," she said. "Everyone's coming. You can be our mascot."

I hesitated for about half a second.

Truth was, I'd never really wanted to be a cheerleader—I'd never even seen a football game. I tried out because it was the quickest path to a normal, disaster-free life I could think of, and that's what I wanted. God wanted it for me too. I was tired of standing apart in the crowded halls of West Junior High.

I was disappointed to be missing out on wearing matching uniforms on game days and blending in with the group, but while the uniform was out, maybe the group was in.

"Count me in!" I high fived Wendy. My new life was beginning.

Chapter 4

Wendy's House o' My Dreams

IF POINT A IS the rec center and Point B is Wendy's house, and the shortest distance between the two is a straight line, I'd say we walked some kind of crazy parabola, stopping at Points C, D, E, and F along the way, points where cute boys happened to live. The universal hope of the cheerleaders was that the boy would be out in the yard tossing around a football or washing their dad's car. Most of them were.

At each point, the girls proclaimed their surprise about making the cheer squad. The depth of their disbelief was unbelievable. I hung back and enjoyed the show, hoping the cute boys would believe I'd made it too. If they noticed me at all.

When we got to Michael Michael's house, the yard was empty.

Lori was shattered because she was in love with him. He was cute enough, but had been thumped on the head with a football one too many times for my taste. Lori refused to budge from the curb without glimpsing his muscles and gaining another opportunity to announce her unsurprising cheerleading success. She made us talk loudly to interrupt his TV program, so he'd come outside.

I backed away from them until I was shielded by a crepe myrtle. The whole thing was kind of embarrassing. They were more than happy for me to keep my distance. I was picking up a vibe that the girls were only humoring Wendy for including me, but Wendy was the queen here, so I wasn't too worried.

Finally, Michael walked out the front door. With him were Ronnie Mills and the aptly named Matt Madewell. Michael and Ronnie were eager to be dazzled by the flashing smiles and fluttering ponytail ribbons of the cheerleaders, but Matt stood back, coolly tossing a baseball in the air and catching it in his glove.

Matt played all the sports, but he'd held onto his brain cells. I loved watching the muscles in his throwing arm bulge and lengthen. We had shared a stand in sixth-grade band during our short and tragic clarinet year—tragic because we both stank at clarinet.

While Michael and Ronnie were bombarded with the miraculous news about cheerleading tryouts, Matt looked over and discovered me hanging out behind the bush. He walked over, tossing the baseball one more time.

"You're doing cheer?" He did a lousy job of hiding his skepticism.

"Actually, no. Turns out I'm as bad at cheer as I am at clarinet."

He snorted. "But you tried out?"

"Yeah," I admitted.

"Weird."

"What's weird about it?"

"I don't know. It's just not you."

"Didn't make it anyway."

"Good! It would ruin you." He winked and tossed the ball in the air.

When the group moved on, with Wendy leading the way, I looked back at Matt. Or more precisely, at his cute butt in his gym shorts.

Did I mention he's aptly named?

Finally, after basically circumnavigating the globe, we arrived at Wendy's house. I could see the rec center from her front lawn.

It was my first time visiting her house. We worked on cheer at the park and consulted on the book report I helped her with on the phone. I knew her family was rich, but I wasn't prepared for how rich.

Her house was straight out of the *Better Homes and Gardens* magazines I browsed in the waiting room of Dr. Weisbein, the orthodontist I went to once a month to be tortured.

It was one of those ranch houses with a two-car garage, orange brick, and brown trim. Beautiful. But the most amazing thing was the Camaro in the driveway; red with an eagle painted on the hood. Flashy for my taste, but still a beauty.

I put on a burst of speed when I realized the girls were on the front porch already.

"Hey, Wendy, whose car?"

"My brother's. Daddy said if he brought his average up to a C, he'd buy it for him, so he did."

She swung open the front door. A thrill fluttered along my spine as I stepped over the threshold. I was about to discover how normal families lived, critical research as I was on my way to joining their ranks.

After I dropped my bookbag in the entryway, the first thing I noticed was the smell of homemade cookies, which was enough to get any girl excited. But when I took a look at the living room, it was like I'd died and gone to Heaven. Before my eyes, the JCPenney catalog came to life. From the u-shaped leisure pit with recliners at both ends to the stained-glass style chandelier with purple bunches of grapes hanging over the five-piece dinette set, it was the house of my dreams. There was even a partly worked jigsaw puzzle on the coffee table.

"It smells amazing in here," I said.

"Momma's a real good cook," Wendy said proudly as Mrs. Walters called from the kitchen.

"Wendy, I made some of those slice-and-bake cookies you like. And I'll zap some pizza rolls too, if you and the girls are hungry."

Mrs. Walters emerged from the kitchen holding a plate of sugar cookies. Her smile faded when she saw me, but she lit it back up. "Brought someone extra, I see. Good thing I made plenty of cookies."

"Thanks, Mom. We'll take those pizza rolls too." Wendy walked past her mom and went straight to the refrigerator.

We each grabbed a can of Cola. Wendy handed me two bags of Nacho Cheese-flavored Corn Chips, and her mom handed me the plate of cookies. I followed the line of girls down the hall, like a rat following the Pied Piper.

Wendy Walters was the luckiest girl on the face of the Earth. She had a canopy bed with a matching dresser and vanity. I ran my finger over the white paint, traced it along the swirls of faux-gold leaf, and sighed. It was exactly like the set on page 237 of the home furnishing section of the *Wish Book*, right down to the purple canopy and bedspread. I'd wished, prayed, and bargained for it, but it never materialized.

On the bedside table sat a pink princess phone with push buttons and Wendy's very own personal phone number. My eyes got misty looking at it.

"Beautiful," I whispered, but nobody heard me.

They were settling down on the shag carpet and passing the chips around like this miraculous room was the most ordinary place they'd ever been. I wanted to lie back on the bed and stare at the canopy, but I knew they'd think I was weird if I did, so I sat on the plush carpet with them. Wendy held court on a purple beanbag.

They talked about the new cheerleading uniforms, what they'd do at summer cheer camp, and what their matching t-shirts should look like. I was sadder than ever that I'd be missing out. And as much as I loved having a glimpse inside Castle Walters, I wondered why Wendy had invited me. There wasn't much I could add to the conversation. It really showed how nice she was, deep down, to ask me over.

Then the topic of conversation turned to what Rhonda had allegedly done with Brandon in the bushes at the graveyard, and things got interesting.

"But Rhonda didn't..." I tried to say before my voice withered under the cutting stares of Stacy and Tracy.

"That's tame stuff," Wendy said. "Look what I've got." She opened the bottom dresser drawer and reached under a stack of winter sweaters. Out came a book. She turned to a dog-eared page in the middle and began to read aloud.

I leaned forward, eyes wide. Everyone did. The book was a thousand times better than Mom's magazines. A nervous thrill made my toes curl every time Wendy said the word "penis." Come Hell or high water, I was going to find that book in the library and check it out. I tilted my head to look past Lori's poofy ponytail so I could see the cover.

Then Wendy paused.

"Don't stop!" we yelled.

Satisfied that she had us in her clutches—as the good Lord clearly intended—a sly smile crossed her face.

"Wait! That's a Judy Blume book." I rose to my knees and reached over Lori and her voluminous hair. Wendy handed me the book. *Forever.* "I thought I'd read all of Judy Blume's books, but I've never seen this in the library."

Wendy lounged luxuriously in her beanbag. "Of course not. They can't put it in school. Too much S. E. X."

"Where'd you get it?" one of the ends-with-y girls asked.

"At the bookstore in the mall."

"Does your mom know?" Lori smirked.

"Hell, no! She never looks at what I buy, just hands over the cash. She trusts me." Her eyes gleamed with naughty joy.

"Read more," said a different ends-with-y girl.

I held the book out to Wendy, pleading with my eyes to hear more.

"No, Guinie, you do it. You're a better reader than I am."

My cheeks got hot. It would be embarrassing to read those words out loud.

But then Lori said, "Yeah, you read it, Guinevere. You're the only person I can stand listening to in English. You even made *The Member of the Wedding* kind of interesting, and that's next door to impossible."

It was the first time Lori Bates Wilson had ever said something nice about me, and I'd known her since kindergarten. So, I read the book. I had to admit, I did have a flair for the dramatic. I put my whole self into it, doing different voices for the boy and the girl. The cheerleaders' breathing was rapid and shallow. I was so into my performance that I didn't notice the door opening.

"Well, I never!" There stood Wendy's mom, holding a plate of pizza rolls, hot from the microwave.

I paused mid-word, which happened to be a word I'd blush to say if Ms. Judy Blume hadn't written it on the page. Mrs. Walters wore a horrified expression. Maybe she'd never heard the word before. She looked at me like I was doggy-doo on the bottom of her shoe. As though I were to blame for the word existing.

The girls gasped.

Wendy squirmed; her lips clamped shut. She gave me a look that said, "Don't tell her it's mine! She'll kill me!"

"Wendy! Kitchen! Now!" Mrs. Walters marched away, taking the pizza rolls with her, which was a shame because a cold pizza roll wasn't worth eating.

Wendy followed without a backward glance.

The girls exhaled in one great gush. They whispered that Wendy was going to get it. They gave me the side eye.

I'd gotten my friend in trouble. The girl who helped me with cheerleading, even though I'm terrible at it, and it's not her fault I didn't make it. I had to save her! Rescue Wendy!

I stepped over Lori and her hair and made for the door.

"No! Don't!" Lori grabbed for my ankle, but I broke free.

"Don't go!"

"Stop!"

The other girls echoed Lori's hissing whispers as if I were charging into the lion's den. But it was no time to think of my personal safety.

I tiptoed down the picture-encrusted hall. The eyes of baby Wendy, holding pom-poms, followed me, urging me to rescue her from being falsely accused. I'd take the blame. Up ahead, Mrs. Walter's voice commanded and demanded so unceasingly that Wendy couldn't get a "but" in crosswise.

When I reached the end of the hall, I heard my name. I stopped in my tracks right next to a picture of preschool Wendy doing the splits.

"She needs to go straight home. You never should have asked her to come over."

For half a second, I dreamed she was talking about someone else, but I couldn't fool myself for long.

"But Mom! I was going to ask if she could stay the night with the other girls."

"The other girls can stay. She has to go."

"But she'll feel bad."

"I don't care. She's not a cheerleader. And more importantly, Guinevere MacKenzie is not a nice girl. She's as abnormal as her mother is. And let me tell you, she's always been an odd one. The whole family's weird. I don't want you hanging around with her."

"But...You don't understand...I need her for...something."

"Not another word, Wendy. Not one."

I tiptoe raced down the hall, biting my bottom lip on the theory that if it hurt enough, I wouldn't feel what was going on inside me.

Not a nice girl.

I stood outside the bedroom door, waiting for Wendy to return, but mainly because I couldn't face the girls inside. What if they thought the same thing: that I wasn't nice? That I was odd. Weird. Not normal. Not like them.

Wendy walked towards me with her head hung low. I took a steadying breath. She looked up and gestured for me to come to her.

"I'm sorry, Guinie," she whispered. "It's my mom. She's such a bitch, but she says everyone has to leave."

I held my breath at the lie. She was probably trying to make me feel better by telling me everyone was in trouble, but it was still a lie. And even though I couldn't have slept over anyway, because it was my dad's weekend, to be ejected and then lied to, made my heart hurt. I didn't call her out, though. As we walked to the front door, I glimpsed her mom opening a fresh box of pizza rolls to zap.

The distance from the house to the street was longer than I remembered. My hopes of becoming normal, miles away.

"Guinevere?"

I turned, hoping she'd changed her mind, that she'd volunteer to tell her mom the truth about the book.

She flashed her best cheerleading smile. "I was wondering. I have this take-home math final to do this weekend. And well, you're so good at math since you go over to the high school to take Algebra and all...." Her words trailed away, but her smile stayed bright.

My shoulders slumped, but what could I do? She was the queen. I held out my hand.

"Oh, thanks. Just a minute." She disappeared into the house for two seconds before reappearing with the test in her hand. "Be sure it's not too good, OK? B-minus will do. See you Monday."

I stuffed the test in my bookbag and walked away with Mrs. Walter's words echoing in my ears, words I knew with painful certainty were true.

Not nice.

Not normal.

Not now.

Not ever.

Chapter 5

Molly is a Friend of Mine

I LEANED AGAINST MRS. Molly Leigh Parmley. Against her gravestone, that is. I hung out with her now and then, when things got to be too much. I never knew her in real life, but her grave was the most private place I knew. It conveniently faced away from the street and was sheltered from view on the other side by a willow tree and flowering bush. If you looked through the leaves, you could see the junior high, home of my triumphs—mainly, going on stage to get my principal's honor roll certificate every quarter—and my disappointments, embarrassments, and humiliations, which were legion.

It was a small cemetery and a little decrepit, kind of like my side of town. And though it was right next to the school sports fields, most of the kids avoided it on account of deep superstition, which made it a great place to go when you needed to get away from the idiocy of your classmates.

Which was often.

I'd gotten to know Molly well.

Which was how I knew the rumors about Rhonda doing it in the graveyard with Brandon were a lie. I was there so often that I would have seen her at least once. She wasn't exactly a saint, but she was way too scared to screw around next to a grave.

I should have spoken up—told those cheerleaders what was what—but I was overwhelmed by the canopy bed. And besides, it would have required telling them my certainty stemmed from hanging out in the cemetery, which would have been complete and utter social suicide.

Though things probably couldn't get worse than they already were.

Luckily, Molly was a great listener. She never gave advice, which was great because even though a person might need advice, they didn't necessarily want it. Sometimes a person just wanted to talk.

She died in 1919, and on her gravestone, it said, "beloved mother," so I was guessing she didn't mind me hanging around. But then again, Wendy's mom was a mother, so maybe my theory about Molly was all wrong.

"What do you think, Molly? Nice or not?"

She didn't answer. Which was a good thing since she was dead.

I looked down at my too-long legs, so pasty white that not even the gajillion freckles speckling them could make me look tan. Shadows from the willow's swaying branches worried over the crusty scab on my shin from a near-fatal shaving accident.

All I could see of myself were those skinny legs, those freckles, that scab, those revolting shoes shedding rubber so fast I'd soon be barefoot. All I could see was the missing pom on my left pompom sock, ripped off and buried in the litter box by my mom's cat, Merlin. All I saw were the royal blue, terry cloth shorts bought at Goodwill, and not as short as they looked; it was only that my legs were long.

From what I saw—that little bit—I had to admit I looked grody. Not neat. Not perfect. Not nice.

But what I knew was, there was a lot more to me than that little bit. That bit was part of a larger picture. I wished Mrs. Walters could see it. I wished everyone could. I wished they would look and realize that Guinevere Galadriel MacKenzie, was greater than the sum of her parts.

I wiped my eyes with the hem of my t-shirt.

From behind Molly's grave, someone moaned, "Oooooo! Wooooo!"

"Guinevere, I'm here for your soul," an eerie voice hissed.

Then, with a giggle and snort, I was tackled from both sides by Susan and Denise.

"Scare ya?" asked Denise.

"Terrified! Can't you tell?"

Susan sat on the headstone next door to Molly's. "How'd it go? Not well, I'm guessing, based on your leaking eyeballs."

"Disaster!"

"You didn't make it? Those bitches."

Denise covered her ears with her hands. "Language."

Susan rolled her eyes. "What happened?"

"What didn't happen? I was so nervous I forgot the cheer and did the funky chicken instead. I assaulted Mr. Randall Bates Wilson with a rubber band. And don't get me started on my cartwheel."

"That bad, huh?"

"Yep, that bad."

Denise was giggling so hard she got the hiccups. "The funky—hic—chicken?"

"I couldn't just stand there. How'd you two find me?"

"We were passing by and saw this headstone had sprouted a ponytail and legs. I'd recognize those ghost-white calves anywhere," said Susan.

"Besides, we know you hang out here," said Denise.

"Yeah, dork, you have no secrets from us."

"You must feel awful."

"Yep. It's not just the tryout, though, it's...well..." I let my sentence die. I didn't want to talk about it, not even with my best friends.

"Well, I'm glad you didn't make it. Means you can join the new pompom squad with me and Denise."

I groaned. "But you don't even have to try out for pom."

"Which means you have a good chance of making the squad," Susan said while Denise giggled and hiccupped all over the place.

"Jerk." I yanked Susan's leg. She fell off the headstone, right on top of Mr. Thomas Perry Parmley.

"Do it, Guinevere. Join pom," Denise managed to say in between giggles and hiccups. "We get to wear our uniforms on game day just like the cheerleaders."

I didn't have the heart to tell her nothing was just like cheerleading, except cheerleading, not if Mrs. Walters had anything to say about it. Still, my interest was piqued. If cheerleading was the most ordinary and normal thing a girl could do, maybe being a pom-pom girl was a close second. I could wear my uniform and blend right into the sea of blue and white on Fridays.

"Do it," Denise urged.

Susan joined Denise in chanting, "Do it. Do it. Do it."

I rested my chin on my hand, posing like that statue of The Thinker, and tried to imagine what pom would be like.

They kept chanting, "Do it. Do it. Do—"

"Stop it already. People will think we're a bunch of sex fiends."

They collapsed into a heap of laughter, teasing each other about being sex-crazed nymphomaniacs.

Susan's thick black hair hung to the middle of her back. She was perpetually tanned and beautiful. Also, great in gym class; she could climb the stupid rope and ring the bell at the top. But some of the boys called her thunder thighs, which is mean and despicable, and when they said it in front of me, I yelled at them, but there was no denying she bought her clothes in the hefty juniors' section.

Denise was such a shrimp that she couldn't shop in the juniors' section yet. She was forced to shop in the girls' department. She didn't even have boobs. Geesh! Delmer Dinkins had bigger boobs than Denise did. But she didn't seem to mind. When someone teased her, she giggled. I didn't know how she did it because when I got teased, I started plotting murder.

If they could do pom, I could do it too, skinny, scabby legs and all. And if I was good at it, it could be a stepping-stone to making cheer the next time I tried out.

"We don't have all day, dork. What's your decision?" Susan demanded.

"I will definitely, positively, very likely, THINK about doing pom."

"You know that means she's going to do it," she said to Denise.

"Yes! She's in!" Denise gave Susan a high five.

"About time, too. I've got to get home. Babysitting tonight." Susan got up and brushed the grass off her behind.

"Ugh! I hate kids. I'll be at my dad's this weekend." I got up and patted the top of the headstone. "Bye, Molly. Thanks for listening."

Denise giggled.

"So weird, Guinevere. So weird." Susan punched me on the shoulder.

We took off walking in different directions, but when I got to the end of the block, I heard Susan shout, "Did I ever tell you you're weird?"

"Jerk," I hollered and waved goodbye.

I couldn't see Denise, but I could hear her giggle echoing down the street.

It was a long walk from the graveyard to my house, and between the two was The Hill.

I paused at the bottom, took a firm grip on the duffle bag that held Wendy's take-home math test, and forced my non-existent muscles to propel me up the near-100% vertical incline.

Once I got to the top where the Catholic church stood, I stood panting until I could breathe—and think—again. There, standing in the shadow of the cross on top of the church's spire, I came to a decision: I would join pom. I'd had a setback, but I couldn't give up my mission to become normal. Pom would be a stop on my path.

At home, I stood on the front porch peering through the battered lace curtain on the narrow window beside the door. Was it safe? As far as I could tell, the coast was clear. But when I opened the door, Merlin bolted out of his hidey hole and swiped at my head, claws out.

"Stupid cat!" There was a fresh scratch on my hairline.

A brute of a Siamese, Merlin scampered to safety with an evil-sounding, "Meowch!" He ran nimbly along the upper platform of the cat palace, which extended from the entryway, where he liked to keep track of the world outside, to the living and dining rooms, where the palace lined the perimeter. Some people had pictures on their walls, but we had tunnels, scratching posts, and cat caves, all covered in plush orange and green carpet. *Better Homes and Gardens*, it was not.

Unfortunately, the combined caterwauling of me and Merlin set off the birds. The quartet of budgies, which I swear are the dumbest birds in existence, were so upset they tossed bird feed out of their cage and onto the floor.

This got the pair of cockatiels going. In their own huge cage, they bobbed their heads and repeated their tiresome phrases.

"Beam me up!"

"Force be with you!"

"Beam me up!"

"Force be with you."

I whistled and whispered in a cheery, sing-song voice to calm them. "Winston, Clementine, take a chill pill. Stupid budgies, shut your beaks or I'll feed you to the cats."

Meanwhile, up by the ceiling, Merlin stalked me, ready to pounce on my head again if I let my guard down.

The orange tabby, Mordred, peered at the birds, licking his lips. I'm sure the wily devil understood me and hoped I'd follow through on my threat.

Gandalf and Uhuru came skittering from the kitchen where their cat chow bowls were always full. Their claws made scratching sounds on the wood floor.

Luckily, the villainous, deaf old Pekingese dog, Morgan le Fay, was nowhere to be seen.

Welcome to the MacKenzie House, where everything was far from ordinary.

Believe it or not, I had no pets of my own. The four cats, one dog, and six birds belonged to my mother, though I did have the distinct privilege and honor of feeding and cleaning up after them. And in case you didn't know, that's sarcasm.

Once, I asked for a guinea pig to call my own, but Mom said guinea pigs smelled bad. When I retorted that we lived in Noah's Ark and nobody would be able to smell a guinea pig over all the other smells, she told me not to be a smart aleck.

"Beam me up. Beam me up."

I couldn't take it anymore. I threw sheets over the cages to calm the birds down. In the kitchen, Mom was cooking dinner. Her hair was in curlers, and she was wearing the blue eyeshadow that signaled a night out.

I scootched behind the card-table kitchenette and shimmied into the chair jammed between the wall and the refrigerator. It was a tight fit, made tighter by the five bowls of animal food on the floor. Luckily, I was skinny.

"You're late," she said.

"I had that thing, remember?"

"What thing?"

"You know. Cheerleading tryouts." Duh.

"Oh. Yeah."

"Aren't you going to ask me?"

"Ask you what?"

I slapped my forehead. Geesh! "Ask me if I made the squad."

"Did you make it?" she said with a startling lack of curiosity.

"No." I covered both eyes with my hands.

"Just as well. I told you we couldn't afford it if you made it. Given that fact, I don't know why you bothered trying out." She plopped a chunk of margarine into the potatoes.

"I've decided to join the pompom squad instead."

She gave the potatoes a violent mash. "We can't afford it, Guinevere."

"Susan and Denise are doing it."

"So, what! I do not have the money. Period! Not while I'm going back to school."

"I'll get Dad to pay for it."

Mom snorted. "Yeah. Right after he pays the 9 ½ years of child support he owes."

"He paid for my braces."

"He made one of the monthly payments. Mamaw paid the rest."

"He probably forgot. I'll ask him when he picks me up tonight."

Mom's strangled sigh escaped into the kitchen. "He's not coming."

"What? Again? Why?"

"Said he had a thing this weekend. Usual excuse."

"What kind of thing?"

"He didn't specify, and I didn't ask." She plopped a gob of potatoes onto a plate.

"This is three times in a row, Mom."

"I know. Believe me, I know. I'm sorry."

I stared blankly into space, trying to push down the anger and tears that threatened to break into the open.

"You'll need to come with me tonight," she said, "I have plans."

My head dropped to the table with the weight of it all. "Where are you going?"

"The Jesus Inn."

I groaned.

"Head up. Dinner is served." Mom placed the plates on the table and unfolded the chair that leaned against the side of the refrigerator when we weren't using it.

I grimaced at the plate. What a failed tryout, an accosting cat, and the knowledge that my dad didn't have time for me couldn't accomplish; my dinner did. I sobbed.

"Liver and onions? You know I hate liver and onions."

Mom pierced a piece of liver with her fork and smiled. "And you know I love them."

Tears rolled down my cheek. "What if I had made cheer? Liver and onions isn't exactly a celebratory dinner, you know. Did you ever think about that?"

"It's a non-issue, Guinevere. You didn't make it, correct?"

"But what if I had?"

"Eat your liver. There are starving kids in Africa who would be grateful for it."

"They can have it," I mumbled as the gross liver gravy seeped into the potatoes, polluting them, making them as rotten as everything else in my life.

That's when I started crying for real.

Mom rested her forehead on her hand. "Guinevere Galadriel, I'm sorry, but..." She sighed.

"Can I stay by myself tonight?"

"No. Mac and cheese. Firemen. Remember?"

Of course, I remembered; she wouldn't let me forget. Mom was at Cherry's place the night it happened. She came home to find two fire trucks and a police car parked in the street with their lights swirling, though they'd turned off the sirens by that time. There wasn't even a real fire. I think the firemen were just bored sitting around the station and wanted to get out.

Anyway, Mom was embarrassed when one of the firefighters talked to her about the house being so cluttered with animals and stacks of books, and junk. Afterward, we went to the hardware store to buy cinder blocks and long boards to make bookshelves. Afterward, I wasn't allowed to stay home by myself anymore. And now there's clutter everywhere again. It's Mom's way.

"I learned my lesson."

"Had to throw that pot away."

"Can I go to Mamaw and Gerald's?"

"You can ask, but it's their square-dancing night."

What a choice: hippie Christians or square-dancing senior citizens. And to think, if I'd been a nice girl, I could have spent the night with Wendy Walters.

Chapter 6

Right and Left Grand Steps to Being Normal

THERE WERE TWO ADVANTAGES of Mamaw living across the street. Number one, when Mom made something disgusting for dinner, I could pick at it and then walk over to see if Mamaw and Grandpa Gerald were eating something better. They almost always were. I say almost, because Mamaw also had an unaccountable fondness for liver and onions. The days their hankering for awful offal synchronized was a sure sign of the approaching apocalypse.

Number two, on nights when Mom was going out and wouldn't let me stay at home because she was still angry about something that happened two whole months earlier, for heaven's sake, I could hang out with my grandparents. They turned the volume on the TV up too loud on account of Mamaw's hearing, but they had cable TV even though Gerald said it was nothing but sex and swearing. I always wanted to ask what was so bad about sex and swearing, but I knew if I did, he'd restrict me to the religious channel for being fresh.

On square dance nights, there was no second dinner or cable TV, but it was better than being with Mom's friends.

When I called, Mamaw said to hurry over because they were fixin' to leave.

Jeans, deodorant, a paperback book, a handful of coins in my pocket, and a spritz of Love's Baby Soft, and I was ready. When I rushed back into the kitchen to scrape my plate, I caught Mom feeding my leftover liver to flat-faced Morgan le Fay. My mother was crooning to the most vicious dog who ever lived, telling it what a "precious poppet" it was.

Revolting.

"Have fun," I called before heading out the door.

Mamaw's house was the largest on the street, but it wasn't fancy, just big. Back when the neighborhood was nothing but a field, she and her first husband built a tiny house by hand; bricks, plumbing, and all. Then over the years, they added a little more here and a little more there.

By the time she married her second husband, Gerald, who was also a builder, the house was big enough, so they bought five tiny houses across the street to rent to people instead. I lived in one of those houses, but we didn't pay rent.

Mom said if it wasn't for Mamaw and Gerald, we'd have to live in a crummy apartment or share a trailer with Cherry, which would be a disaster because it would also mean sharing a trailer with Cherry's weirdo son, Timmy.

When I walked outside, Mamaw and Gerald were in the driveway waiting for me. They were dressed to the hilt in their fancy dance clothes. Mamaw made them. She sewed Gerald's shirts in the same fabric as her dress so that when the Square Dance Caller said to take your partner and do-si-do, there was no confusion about who belonged to whom.

The skirt of Mamaw's dress was a full circle with layers and layers of petticoats underneath, making it stick out like an open umbrella.

"Spin, Mamaw. Show off your funny panties."

Her eyes sparkled as she spun right in the driveway for the whole neighborhood to see. The skirt and petticoats twirled higher and higher until you could see her bloomers underneath. They were like tight shorts with rows of lace covering them. I knew it was weird to call them funny panties, but I started calling them that when I was a little kid, and the name stuck.

When she stopped spinning, she wasn't even dizzy. With a laugh, she pulled me in for a hug. "Sorry your dad's such a loser."

"He's not a loser. He had a thing."

She looked over at Gerald and raised her eyebrow. "The only thing he has is irresponsibility." She said it like she was warning me, like irresponsibility might be contagious. Then she shook her head. "Fawn always has been able to pick 'em."

I shrugged. Irresponsible or not, he was still my dad. But I didn't talk back to Mamaw because she was my Mamaw.

"You ready to square dance, G?" Grandpa Gerald asked.

"No, but I'm ready to watch."

"Then climb on into this truck."

Getting into the pickup required a combination of pulling, climbing, and jumping. And while I'd never once managed to get even halfway up the stupid rope in gym class, I managed the truck.

I always sat in the middle with my knees drawn up and my feet on the hump in the center. On square dance night, it was essential. If Mamaw sat in the middle, Grandpa Gerald couldn't see to drive—her skirt and petticoat were that big.

The best thing about sitting in the middle was controlling the music. I popped Conway Twitty out of the 8-track player & popped Debby Boone in as the best of the bad options. It was all country all the time with the grands, though Gerald liked a bit of classical music now and then—a cultured heart in a rugged exterior. I sang along to "You Light Up My Life" and he joined in on the chorus, the two of us squealing like feedback on the CB radio he had installed on the dashboard.

Mamaw covered her ears. "Land's sake. You all are butchering this beautiful song. I'm about to blow your candles out."

After the harsh critique, we tried to soldier on, but our duet petered out in a round of laughter. Debby Boone moved on to singing "A Rock and Roll Song," which was the least rock-n-roll thing I'd ever heard, but I liked it anyway.

The beige, cinder block community hall where the square dancers danced was filled to overflowing with color as the women in their jewel-tone dresses and men in matching pearl-snap shirts greeted each other. For a bunch of old folks, they sure had fun.

And they were old. Some were older than Mamaw, and she was already 50. She was 17 when she had my mom's big brother, and Mom had me when she was 17. I was 14 and it made me nervous. There was no way I would be responsible enough to have a baby in three more years. I couldn't even shave my legs without scraping the skin off my shins and bleeding all over the bathtub.

I stuck close to Gerald as he carried a tray of pimento cheese sandwiches to the refreshment table and picked up my fair share of teasing along the way, including a little cheek-pinching, but only as a joke.

One of Gerald's friends, Max, was already on his second glass of punch. It was nonalcoholic, but cranberry juice and lemon-lime soda have a funny effect on some people. He gently pinched my cheek. "You going to cut a rug with us, young lady?"

"Not tonight. I don't want to show you up. I got an A in square dancing at school, you know."

Laughter ensued, as I'd intended, but it was true. It was the only time I got an A in gym.

I grabbed two of the sandwiches since I hadn't had a decent dinner, and with a backward wave, left the hall as the Square Dance Caller called the dancers to their squares.

The lobby of the community center was deserted, with nothing but the muted thump of soft-soled feet and swish of petticoats to remind me I wasn't alone. It was quiet enough for a phone call.

I dug coins out of my jeans pocket, lined the quarters up on the ledge of the payphone, plunked the first in line into the slot, and dialed Susan's number one digit at a time, waiting for the dial to rotate around the circle before dialing the next.

"Jackson residence." In the background, her brothers and sisters made a racket. They were a noisy family, but there were about a million of them, so it made sense.

"Hello. This is the payphone at the Central Park Community Center calling for Miss Susan Jackson."

"Ya got her, bub." She snort-laughed. "I thought you were going to your dad's."

"Change of plans."

"Again?"

"Yep. Hey, I was wondering. How much does pom cost?"

"Are you going to do it? Please say yes."

"Depends. How much does it cost?"

"Two, twenty-five, but it includes everything. The skirt, two different tops, shoes, socks, pompoms, coaching. Everything."

"Two *hundred* twenty-five? You're kidding. How am I going to come up with that kind of dough?"

"How were you going to pay for cheer? It costs more."

"Didn't really think about it. Guess I was hoping a rich uncle would die or something."

"You're weird, Guinevere."

"It's my fatal flaw. How are you paying for pom?" Susan was as poor as I was, maybe poorer because her family was huge.

"Babysitting."

"Ugh. I'm not even allowed to babysit myself. Besides, I hate children."

"But it pays well."

The robot operator broke into the line, "Please deposit twenty-five cents to continue the call."

"Wait, wait, I've got it." I slipped the next quarter into the slot. "Where was I? Oh yeah, I'll babysit maybe as a very—extremely—last resort. I'll figure something out."

"They said if you sew your own skirt and one of the tops, it costs less. Like $190 or something."

"I can sew! I got an A in Home Ec and everything."

"Wish I could. It would mean one less babysitting job. I barely squeaked a C in sewing, though."

"Yeah. I remember that skirt you made."

"Hey, I've got to go before my siblings tear the house down."

"Good luck!"

"I'm gonna need it."

Click

I hung the handset on the receiver, stuffed the remaining quarters into my jeans pocket, and slumped into a vinyl chair.

"Right and left grand," the Caller sang.

How much longer? I couldn't believe those oldsters were still going strong. What was the world coming to? Old people should be home in their rocking chairs instead of dancing the night away. My grandparents had a better social life than I did.

I closed my eyes and leaned my head on the back of the chair. $225 or $190, it didn't matter. I was flat broke.

Like an angel, Scott Baio appeared on the back of my eyelids. He looked exactly like he did on the biggest poster over my bed.

"How would you get the money, Scott?"

He smiled at me with all his perfect teeth. "Why, I'd just star in another TV show."

"You're no help, Scott."

But then my eyes popped open. "Great idea, Scott."

Nobody would hire me to be on a TV show, but they might hire me for something besides babysitting. The plus side was that getting a job was as normal as normal could be. It totally fit into my plan, the details of which came into focus as I thought about it. Plan A—cheerleading—hadn't worked out. Plan B would be much more methodical.

Mom was still out when we finally got home, so I spent the night with the grands. Their guest room was kind of a second bedroom for me. I slipped into the soft old nightgown that Mamaw kept ready in the top drawer and sat cross-legged on the bed with a pad of paper and pencil in hand to map out my plan of attack.

My list was inspired by the lists I'd seen in Mom's magazines, like "10 Easy Steps to Get a Man" or "10 Ways to Lose Weight for Good." Mine said:

<u>*10 Easy Steps to Becoming Normal*</u>

1. *Join Pom.*

a.   Let's face it, pom isn't cheerleading, but it's the next best thing. It has all the essentials for fitting in with the crowd: blue and white uniforms, cute, sweaty football players (one in particular), and Friday night games that everyone except the Stoners goes to.

b.   If I'm good at it—what am I saying? WHEN I'm good at it—I'll try out for cheerleading again next year.

2.   Get a job.

a.   To pay for pom.

```
    i.        Ice cream scooper?
    ii.       Grocery store?
    iii.      Mow lawns? (No!)
    iv.       Babysit? (Not on your life!)
    v.        Mamaw????
```

3.   Become best friends with Wendy Walters.

a.   No explanation needed.

4.   Convince Mom and Dad to be less weird.

a.   Nothing is impossible, right? It says so in the Bible or the Constitution or something.

5.   Improve my wardrobe.

a.   How?

i.   Seeing as how I'll probably need every penny I earn at my job (see #2) to pay for pom (see #1), this seems almost as impossible as getting the parents to be less weird (#4).

ii.   Maybe I can get a job at a department store?! I hear they give discounts if you work there.

1.   *Do department stores hire 14-year-olds?*

6.   *Get a personality transplant.*

a.   Let's face it, you're bonkers. Everyone knows it.

i.   Don't I wish there was such a thing?! A pill, a button, a pod like in *Invasion of the Body Snatchers*. Unfortunately, this will require serious work.

7.   *Find a boyfriend.*

a.   Wendy has a boyfriend, or she will soon if Ronnie Mills knows what's good for him. All the normal girls on TV and in the magazines have one. I should, too.

```
    i.         Scott Baio is taken, and
Joanie looks like she can lay me out.
    ii.          Would  Matt  Madewell
ask  me  out?  He  is  made  well.
(Hardy-har-har).
```

8. *Get my braces off.*

a.   Of all the weird things about me, this is the most normal, but does Dr. Weisbein have to be so creative with the rubber band patterns?
b.   For this to happen, I need to actually wear my rubber bands (see above).

9. *Makeup? Perfume? Just the right soap? A better shampoo?*

a.   Calgon, take me away.

10. *Pray.*

If I could get the first five done, I'd be halfway there.

Literally.

If I could get the first five done, it would be nothing short of a miracle.

Chapter 7
Working 9 to 5

WHEN I WOKE UP Saturday morning in Mamaw's spare bed, I remembered that Dad had promised we'd go to a movie that day. He'd promised to make goulash, which he served so often that I wondered if he ate it every night, even when I wasn't there. I was disappointed about the movie, not about the goulash.

But then I spotted my list on the bedside table.

Seeing as I still needed about two hundred dollars to achieve the first step on my list, I had no time to wallow in disappointment.

The beautiful smell of pancakes and bacon filled the kitchen.

"Morning." I playfully tugged Mamaw's apron ties as she stood at the stove, waiting to flip over the pancakes.

She gave me a peck on the cheek. "Breakfast is about ready. Go get Gerald, won't you?"

Grandpa Gerald was out back in his workshop. I stood at the back door and yelled, "Gerald! Breakfast!" and he popped out, dusting the wood chips off the white overalls he wore every weekend. They were splattered with many colors of interior and exterior house paint, but the white parts gleamed. I suspected Mamaw ironed them.

At the breakfast table, Mamaw pushed plenty of bacon my way. She thought I was too skinny, except for my boobs. It's why she was always willing to feed me when Mom made something disgusting or decided to go on yet another diet.

I snatched an extra crispy strip. "Where can I get a job? I need money. Lots of money. Do you think Warehouse Market might hire me to bag groceries? Or maybe Braums? I could scoop ice cream."

Gerald chased the bacon with a swig of coffee before saying, "Don't know. There's a lot of rules around hiring someone younger than sixteen. Some places don't want to deal with it."

"How much money do you need?" Mamaw asked.

"About $200."

"What in the world do you need $200 for?"

"I want to sign up for the pompom squad. It's kind of like cheerleading, but cheaper, believe it or not. I'll get to wave my pompoms at all the football games."

She eyed me skeptically as she chewed. Then I brought home the zinger.

"You know, like all the nice girls at school."

I knew her two natures were warring inside her, like an angel and a devil duking it out. The angel was so frugal and saving as to be downright cheap. But the devil was interested in how things "looked." It drove her crazy that my mom was far out in another galaxy from how most people acted.

Grandpa Gerald winked at me. He knew I was angling—and he knew Mamaw.

I sat patiently, chomping my bacon and imagining the angel and devil arguing with each other.

ANGEL: That's a lot of money to be spending on something as pointless as pompoms.

DEVIL: But the nice girls are doing it. Wouldn't it be good for Guinevere to have a positive influence in her life?

ANGEL: It wouldn't look good to spend all that and have her parade around in a short skirt. What would the ladies at church say?

DEVIL: Well, it looks worse that she's growing up with weirdo parents.

In the end, Gerald was my angel. "Don't you need some help, Juanita? It'd be cheaper to hire G than anyone else."

A huge smile crossed her face. The angel and devil could both win. She'd help me join the nice girls, which would look good, but she'd pay me a fraction of what anyone else would. I knew it, but the second she offered me $40 to clean her shower that very day, I said yes. Blinded by the bucks.

"How soon can I start?"

It took two and a half hours of continuous labor to clean the shower, a big walk-in with tiny, white porcelain tile on the floor, up the walls, and on the ceiling. I used a toothbrush to scrub every grout line. I knew she would check because she liked to get her money's worth. I stayed focused on the $40 and belted out Olivia Newton-John's greatest hits while I scrubbed. "Xanadu" sounded great in there because of the echoes.

By the time I finished, I was wet from head to toe on account of using the shower head to rinse the tile while I was still in the shower, which was the only way to do it right.

When she paid me, I asked if I could clean the shower again tomorrow. But she said it only needed a deep clean about once a month, which was a bummer. However, she said if I came back after church on Sunday, she'd think of other things I could do. I took it as a hint to go home.

Mom was sitting at the kitchen table in her housecoat, reading one of her college textbooks. Morgan le Fay was on her lap. The beast snarled at me. Stupid dog.

"Hey, Mom. Is there anything I can do around here to earn money?"

"You live here. I'm not paying you to do what you should do for free."

"But..."

"For heaven's sake, go play. I need to study for finals."

I didn't play, but I did go away.

I changed into something kind of foxy because I had places to go, errands to run. And I hoped I'd bump into Matt Madewell. I read in Cosmo that you should be prepared to see people when you leave the house because if you went out looking like something the cat dragged in, you were guaranteed to see everyone you knew.

I added my earnings to my savings: $40.00 + $15.71 = $55.71. With a pang of regret, I tucked $10 into my pocket for a good cause. Research. I was certain the investment would pay off in the end.

I walked the mile to the local library. It seemed like I walked another mile through the aisles looking for a book telling me how to be normal, but a thorough search turned up no such title. Once I became normal, I'd have to write it myself.

The librarian was at her desk stamping in returned books. Her name was Charlene, and she was working at the library to pay for a master's degree in library science. It seemed to me that she was already doing what she wanted without going to school, but what did I know? Anyway, Charlene knew me pretty well because I came to the library a lot.

Her eyes sparkled when she saw me. You'd be surprised how few kids my age came in to check out books.

"How did you like *Jane Eyre*?"

"I loved it. I especially loved the whole mad wife in the attic thing. I didn't see it coming. But I did wonder why Jane didn't marry St. John Rivers. He seemed nice and stable, like he was going places. Rochester seemed risky to me. You never know with a man like that. He might not be going anywhere at all."

The sparkle in her eyes faded a bit. I didn't know why. "What can I help you find today?" she asked.

"I'm looking for a how-to guide. For research. How to be normal."

All the joy went out of her eyes." You know there's no such thing as normal, right?"

I barely managed to keep my eyes from rolling. Master's degree or not, Charlene had no idea what she was talking about. "Well, how about books normal girls read, then?"

"Guinevere, you don't have to dumb yourself down."

"Yeah, I know. How about books *most* girls read?"

"A lot of girls your age like Judy Blume. And *P.S. I Love You* has been so popular, we had to order another copy."

I'd read them, but I hadn't studied them for clues about how normal people lived. I would start with those. Especially if they had...

"Do you have *Forever* by Judy Blume?"

Her eyebrow rose above her eyeglass frame. "That one we don't carry."

"Too bad. I'd like to know how it ends." Who was I kidding? I was only interested in the sexy parts.

"We have a whole section of teen paperbacks. Let me show you."

And so, I loaded my duffel with paperbacks and headed down the road to QuikTrip.

I hadn't seen Matt yet, but I hadn't expected him to be at the library. He's smart, but he has better things to do than hang out among books on Saturday afternoon. Unfortunately, he wasn't at QT either. Michael Michaels was there, though, so my efforts to look nice weren't completely wasted. Michael might tell Matt he saw me. Then Matt might ask how I looked. And even though Michael probably wouldn't tell Matt I looked foxy, he might at least say I didn't look too bad.

I bought three magazines: *Seventeen*, *Teen*, and *Tiger Beat*. The *Tiger Beat* wasn't part of my research, but because it had a very cute picture of Scott Baio on the cover, along with a pull-out poster I could add to the collage above my bed.

I also bought a root beer slushie and a candy bar, which had nothing to do with my research but everything to do with the fact that I liked them.

Back at home, I closed the door and cleaned my already clean room because Lemon Pledge put me in the mood for thinking. The cats poked their paws under the door.

"Fat chance, kitties. You've got the rest of the house. This is mine."

Then I sat on the floor of my clean, cat-free, non-chaotic room and spread my research materials on the floor: two teen magazines, the library books, the JCPenney catalog, and the *TV Guide* in which I had circled all the shows depicting the life of the normal American teenage girl. Those would be my textbook. My how-to guide for being perfectly normal.

And this time, I wouldn't fail.

Chapter 8

In the Land of the Blind, the One-Eyed Man is King

THE FINAL FEW DAYS of eighth grade were so dreadful, they nearly convinced me that there was no hope; I'd be abnormal forever. I held my head up, though, remembering The Call I'd heard that night at The Jesus Inn. Better days were ahead. My plans were just getting started.

On Monday, Wendy and the newly christened 1981-82 Freshman Cheer Squad showed up in the matching t-shirts they'd painted at the sleepover, making Wendy's lie glaringly obvious.

At lunch, Lori Bates Wilson reenacted my disastrous tryout, including flicking a rubber band at Michael for the finale. Mrs. Walters had told them all about it. Judging by the laughter, Lori's performance was a smash hit with her audience.

It wasn't a big hit with me. But when Wendy put her arm around my shoulder and said, "Don't be mad, Guinie. It's funny," I held my peace. Becoming her best friend was number three on my list. Without her approval, I'd be stuck in the ranks of the weird forever.

Like the sap I am, I gave her the math test I completed for her. She got a B-minus. If I'd let her get an A, the math teacher would have known something fishy was going on. And the more I learned about the ecosystem I was living in, the more certain I was that being found out as a cheat would weigh heavier on me than it would on Wendy. Those were the rules of the jungle at West Junior High.

At the end of the year awards assembly, I got certificates for the principal's honor roll, perfect attendance, and Math Team, plus a tiny trophy for winning the spelling bee. Wendy got huge trophies for "Most Spirited" and "Most Likely to Succeed" in ninth grade and life.

The only thing that helped me survive those last days was the knowledge that I was studying my homemade textbook and working the plan. Come August and the first day of Freshman Year, I'd blow everyone away with my transformation.

And I can't forget to mention that Susan and Denise helped too. They were the best, best friends anyone could have. When I became best friends with Wendy, I was going to take them along with me. They just didn't know it yet.

Oh, and Matt did a lot to help me survive. When Lori was making fun of me, she overheard Matt telling Michael, "Looks like Lori needs some Meow Mix. Too bad the bar-feteria doesn't serve it."

And Lori almost cried because Michael laughed at Matt's suggestion that she was being catty, almost like he agreed with it. She's in love with Michael, so it hit hard.

When Matt and I got our certificates for Math Team, he high-fived me.

Also, after the final bell of the year rang at 3:00, making my class the new Queens and Kings of the school, I saw Matt in the hall. He said he'd see me at the park pool. It was possibly going to be a summer of transformation in more ways than one.

It made me so happy that I joined the chant of "We rule the school," even though I knew the truth; it was ruled by Wendy's mother.

Segue to Thursday and the first day of pom practice, outside the rec center, over by the picnic tables.

Boy was I right when I said it wouldn't be like cheerleading. As I approached the meeting place, I had to remind myself that pom was number one on my "10 Ways to Be Normal" list and that I was slaving away at Mamaw's, earning paltry pennies from her frugal fingers to pay for it. I needed to stay focused, tamp down the urge to turn around, go home, and sit in front of the idiot box, which is what Mom called the TV.

The squad consisted of plus-sized Susan, pocket-sized Denise, and beanpole-with-boobs me. There was also taller-than-the-principal Jerica, and Charity Louise with her culottes and religious tracts.

The cherry on top was Tonya "never met a boy she didn't like" Hubner. She wore enough eyeliner to circle the Earth three times. Her mother was rumored to dance at the Yellow Brick Road Bar and Grill, though I'm not judging because my dad was a bartender, and my mom's best friend worked at a head shop. I'm just pointing out where Tonya's mom may or may not have worked to demonstrate that our group was absolutely, positively, definitely nothing like the cheerleaders.

There wasn't one girl whose name ended in y.

Coach Jamey's eyes swept over us. Her name did, obviously, end in y, but it didn't count because she wasn't one of us. I gave her credit for disguising the disappointment in her eyes with a perky smile. Although she had just tucked our checks to pay for pom into her purse, which may have had something to do with it.

She told us she had just finished her first year in junior college. "It's great, girls. Much better than high school, and much, much better than junior high, which is the worst."

I agreed. Everything was better than junior high, except maybe liver and onions.

Coach Jamey was a very bubbly, smiling kind of person. Even though I suspected she was disappointed that we weren't like the cheerleaders, I couldn't help but like her.

"Junior college is where I learned about pompom dance squad. I loved cheerleading in high school, but pom is even more fun. It's kind of new to this side of town, but I think you'll really like performing on the field at halftime. And the crowd will like it to—once they embrace the newness of it."

"So, we get to dance? On the football field?" Tonya asked as she unscrewed the top of her roll-on lip gloss.

"Yes! Isn't it exciting?!" Jamey bubbled.

"Surprisingly, yes," Tonya answered.

Charity Louise looked worried. I wouldn't be surprised if dancing was on her very long list of sinful activities.

I was a little worried too, and it had nothing to do with sin. Dancing on the football field wasn't what I'd expected. Pom was veering dangerously away from normal. Cheerleaders stayed on the sidelines. But Mamaw had advanced me the money, and I'd already turned it over, so I decided to keep an open mind.

"Now, I was hoping to have a couple more girls on the squad because it makes the pompom passes more thrilling!"

She made pompom passes sound exciting. I couldn't wait to find out what they were.

"So, if you have friends who want to join, tell them it's not too late. OK?" She smiled with all her straight, white teeth.

I smiled back, under her spell. Unfortunately, I was fresh out of friends to recruit. Susan and Denise were already here, and I didn't think Wendy would give up cheer to join us.

"Ready?!" she said like she was going to do a cheer. "Let's play a game to get to know each other better."

Tonya sat at her own table so we nerds wouldn't pollute her air. Even from a distance, I could smell the Wicked Watermelon lip gloss she'd smeared on her lips. It smelled fantastic, and it made her lips sparkle like they were coated with crushed up diamonds. I wanted to ask her where she got it and how much it cost, but not yet because she looked annoyed.

"We've been going to school together since kinder-garten," she said, picking a strand of bleached blond hair off her glossy lips. "We already know each other. For in-stance, I know Guinevere's read every book in the library but has never kissed a boy. And I know if Charity Louise tries to 'save' me one more time, I'm going to flush those tracts down the toilet."

Charity Louise slid a tract back into her pocket.

I covered my face with my hands, embarrassed that Coach Jamey had discovered my failings.

But Jerica stood up, towering over Tonya. "And we know you think you made the sun and hung it, but you never did. So why don't you sit there and listen to Coach?"

Tonya clamped her sparkling lips shut.

Jerica sat down like nothing had happened, and Coach gave her a grateful smile. We played the game.

It went like this: each person had to tell two true things about themselves and one lie, and the rest of us had to guess which was which. Charity Louise pursed her lips at the thought of lying.

Susan volunteered to go first, but she turned to me and Denise. "You two, keep quiet."

We zipped our lips.

"I'm a princess. I love babysitting. I got sugarless gum and a calorie counter in my Christmas stocking."

I itched to tell, but Susan was right, I had an unfair advantage. Denise put her head under the table so she wouldn't be tempted to say the answer. We could all hear her giggling.

"You're not a princess, that's for sure, living over in the trailer park," Tonya scoffed.

"Where you live, too," Susan added.

"Exactly. That's the lie. What do you think, Charity Louise? Jerica?"

"I'm not sure," said Jerica. "Who in their right mind gives their kid a calorie counter for Christmas?"

Denise's giggles had given her the hiccups. "Hold your breath," I whispered.

Charity Louise warmed to the game. "I think Tonya's right. There aren't any princesses in America."

"Majority rule." Jerica threw up her hands.

"Wrong!" I blurted.

Susan smiled. "Wrong. I'm an Indian Princess for my tribe. It's kind of like being Miss America. I have a crown and everything."

"She's right. She's right." Denise emerged from under the table. "I've seen it."

"Which is the lie?" asked Coach Jamey.

"Babysitting. The only thing I like about it is the money."

"I'll go next," said Charity Louise. "I've been baptized three times just to be safe. I was voted most likely to be a missionary at Bible Camp. I love Jesus with all my heart."

I tilted my head. We all did, even Coach, and she'd just met Charity Louise.

"But those things are all true," I said.

"Of course they are. I can't tell a lie. It's not Christian."

"You're missing the point," said Susan.

"It's a game, doofus!" said Tonya. "I'll go next. I saw Rhonda and Brandon do it in the bushes in the graveyard. Maybelline is better than Cover Girl. I've covered all the bases."

Charity Louise gasped. Her hand shook as she pushed a tract across the picnic table in Tonya's direction.

I spoke up like I wished I'd done with the cheerleaders. "Rhonda never did anything in the graveyard. That's the lie."

"How do you know?"

Jerica stood up again. "I know because Rhonda is my friend. You didn't see anything, so you better shut your mouth about her."

Tonya flipped her hair. "Alright, then. That's the lie. I didn't see anything, but that doesn't mean it didn't happen. Everyone's talking about it."

Coach Jamey gently put her hand on Jerica's elbow to restrain her. "Isn't this illuminating?"

She looked like coaching om was turning out to be more than she expected. I'm guessing that when she signed up, she didn't imagine there'd be this much sex and violence.

The rest of us tried not to look at Tonya because if the gossip about Rhonda was the lie, it meant Tonya had made a homerun. And while we might have suspected it, hearing it right out in the open like that was embarrassing.

"My turn," I said, breaking the tension. "My dad has met sixteen celebrities, including Peter Frampton and Linda Ronstadt. I hear Soviet spies broadcasting through my braces. I popped Mr. Randolph Bates Wilson with a rubber band."

Coach gave me a thumbs up and a relieved smile.

"Your dad doesn't know Linda Ronstadt," said Tonya.

"Can you really hear the Soviets?" Denise asked, her eyes wide.

Jerica laughed. "I wish somebody would pop that man with something, but no way you did that."

Susan's the one who got it right. She knew about the rubber band incident, and I'd told her about the people Dad met at the country club where he bartended. All the musicians went there to have a drink after their shows when they came to Tulsa on tour. With those being true, it meant I couldn't hear the Soviets, though sometimes I did pick up the local radio station.

I learned that Jerica hated basketball and hated that everyone thought she should play because she's so tall. I learned that Coach Jamey was pre-engaged to a boy she met in one of her college classes. And even though I thought I knew everything about Denise, I learned that her brother is thirty-five years old, which means he's older than my mom, and Denise's old parents are more ancient than I thought they were.

After the game, we spent the next hour passing pom-poms over our heads, between our legs, from side to side, and back. It wasn't as easy as it sounds. Those masses of blue and white plastic on sticks were heavier than they looked.

Once we'd gotten the hang of the basics, Coach popped a cassette tape into a portable tape player, and we practiced passing the pompoms in time to "Funkytown."

I was bad at gym and terrible at clarinet, but I had good rhythm. And when we added dance moves and hip swings to the passes, I realized I was a natural.

"Great job, Guinevere! Shake it!" Coach Jamey looked relieved because—let's just say—the others still had a lot to learn.

Denise couldn't keep the beat. Charity Louise's culottes got in the way. Tonya dropped the pompoms every time a boy walked by. Or biked by. Or was within a quarter mile of us. Susan and Jerica grasped the skill but were having so much fun, they couldn't stop goofing off.

As I danced and Coach beamed at me, I knew that even though it wasn't cheer, I'd found something I was good at. Guinevere MacKenzie was good at something halfway normal.

I've heard it said that in the land of the blind, the one-eyed man is king. I was that one-eyed man—or woman, thank you very much. I wasn't normal yet. It would probably take all summer until I was. But when it came to pom, I was the queen.

Chapter 9

The Tide is High, so Don't Do Me Like That

THE TEEN MAGAZINES GAVE all kinds of advice about going to the pool, from how to do your hair to what kind of suit to wear to which mascara would stand up to a dunking. What they didn't tell you is what to do when you get your period on the morning the park pool opened for the summer, a day that everyone who mattered would be there. Matt Madewell would be there. I hadn't seen him for a whole week, not since the last day of school when he told me he'd see me at the pool. It was the closest I'd ever gotten to being asked on a date.

Even Judy Blume let me down. She tackled a lot of problems in her books, but not once did she tell you what to do when pool opening day coincided with the pimple that showed up on the right side of your nose every time you got your period. And she said nothing about what to do when the cute purple swimsuit you bought at a garage sale in that swanky neighborhood was lower cut in the area of the bosom than you expected.

The only solution I thought of was to wear shorts over my suit—and maybe a scarf.

The cherry on top of the crap sundae was that Dr. Weisbein got extra-creative in the rubber band design he thought up for my teeth: four crisscrossing bands. I could barely open my mouth.

I was doomed.

Mom had a class before she went to work, so she agreed to drop me off on the way. The Swoosh Mobile stalled twice on the way there, though, so it might have been faster to walk. By the time I arrived, the gates were open, and the pool was churning with bodies.

There was no line at the payment window. On the other side of it, the workers were gasping for air and looking frazzled like they'd just been through a war. The first day of pool season could do that to you. One of them looked up and audibly sighed when she saw me, but another bounded off the desk he was sitting on like it had given him an electric shock.

He was wearing a junior college t-shirt and muscles. He swaggered like he was hot stuff.

I should have worn that scarf. Or a parka.

"What would you like today, little lady?"

I squatted down so our eyes were on the same plane. He seemed surprised to discover I had eyes. That I was not, in fact, a pair of disembodied boobs.

"It's a pool. What do you think I want?" I handed him my punch card. Mom wouldn't pay for pom, but she forked over $25 for a summer pool pass, mainly because it got me out of her hair.

He punched the card. "That purple suit looks nice with your hair." He winked.

I turned my back on him and flipped my towel over my shoulder before looking back to glare at him. "Just so you know. I'm only fourteen and two months." I said it through clenched teeth, which made me sound tough, but it was only because I couldn't open my mouth all the way. I tried not to swing my hips when I walked to the pool.

Luckily, Susan and Denise were easy to find. They had claimed a spot next to the chain link fence by spreading their towels out on the concrete, leaving a space in the middle for me.

"Finally! What took you so long?" said Susan.

Denise bounced on her knees as I flicked my towel and watched it drift into the empty spot.

"You forgot to shower," she said. "Remember, you have to shower before you get in the pool."

She wore a bikini covered with little strawberries. It was cute. The band top went straight across her chest with no gaps or bumps. Must be nice.

When I sat cross-legged on my towel with my shorts still on, she took one look at my low-cut suit and then at her chest.

"I don't think my bust exercises are working," she muttered.

"You look cute. Perfect. And I didn't shower because I'm not swimming."

"What?"

"Why?"

They groaned.

I whispered, "Period."

"Oh, man!" Denise hadn't got hers, but Susan and I moaned so much about ours that it made her wish she never would.

Susan leaned over to whisper in my ear. "I have a tampon in my bag."

"No," I whined. "I hate them." I pouted. "I'd rather just sit here and be miserable than use one of those things."

I stuck my bottom lip out and crossed my arms over my chest.

"Someone's hormones are out of whack."

Denise giggled.

"We won't swim either. We'll all sunbathe. I've been meaning to work on my tan." Susan had a gorgeous twelve-month tan, but I appreciated the solidarity.

Denise did not. She collapsed back on her towel like she'd fainted. "Dumb period. I've been dying to swim."

I looked at Susan. "Go swim before Denise starts crying. I'll be fine."

"Yay!" Denise popped up. "Come on, Suzy-Q!"

Susan tossed her t-shirt to me. "If your chest starts burning, you can cover it with that." She laughed a throaty laugh. If she weren't my friend, I wouldn't have known she was joking. But she was, and I did.

I watched them walk down the side of the pool to the deep end, Denise in her little girl's bikini and Susan in her cutoffs and tank top. To get the size of swimsuit she needed, she had to shop in the women's department where all the swimsuits looked like something Mamaw would wear. She was saving her money until she lost weight and could buy something cute.

They joined Jerica and her friend Rhonda, subject of the nefarious graveyard rumor. Jerica and Susan were planning to gang up on her and get her to join pom so our pompom passes would be more spectacular.

Denise did handstands and somersaults in the water while the other three held onto the side of the pool and talked.

I hoped Rhonda would join the squad because it would make Coach Jamey happy. I talked to Coach after practice one day when the other girls left. She was concerned Tonya might not make it to homecoming, implying that she might end up in the family way. That didn't worry me too much because, having known Tonya forever, I suspected she talked bigger than she acted. However, I did think there was a risk that she might get bored and quit. I crossed my fingers and prayed that Jerica and Susan could convince Rhonda.

It was cool talking to Jamey that day. She said I was really good at pom and that I should consider going to junior college after high school because she thought I'd do really great. I told her my mom went to the junior college, but she was an adult learning student. Jamey said it was brave of my mom to go back to school. I guess maybe it was.

Outside of the fenced-in pool area, a boy and a girl were making out on a park bench. They were all arms and legs, but judging by the way the sun glinted off the girl's lip gloss, I was pretty sure it was Tonya. The boy looked like he was about to hit a home run.

Geesh!

Maybe Coach Jamey wasn't wrong about Tonya making it to homecoming.

Wendy and the cheerleaders were hanging out with the usual suspects—the football players, or was it baseball now? I lost track of the seasons, but it was the same group of guys.

Ronnie Mills was trying to dunk Wendy. It was so romantic. Everyone knew they'd been practically engaged since birth; their mothers told anyone who would listen. Wendy looked annoyed, but I think it was because her hair looked so good.

I waved at her when she looked my way, but I don't think she saw me.

There were other people there too, of course. The kids who stuck with band for more than one year. The little kids. The little kids' mothers taking regular peeks at the hunky lifeguards.

While I observed all of this, including the lifeguards, Matt Madewell plopped down next to me on Denise's old Raggedy Ann towel.

Have I mentioned that he and his name were completely simpatico? How the blonde hairs on his legs caught the light of the sun and refracted it into a rainbow of foxiness?

"Not swimming?" Water droplets clung to his eyelashes, which were rather long.

I looked at him kind of sideways because if I looked straight on, he was sure to notice the zit on my nose.

"No. Just soaking up the sun."

"That's cool."

Every other boy I knew would have taken in my non-swimming status and the shorts I wore over my suit, and made a comment like, "'Cause you're on the rag." But not Matt. He let it go. It was one of the many things that made him totally awesome.

"Good summer so far?" he asked.

"Yeah. All one week of it. What about you?"

"First week has been good. Mainly just helping my dad in his auto shop."

"Whoa. Déjà vu." In my excitement, I turned to look at him full on and noticed he had a zit on his nose, too. "I've been working for my grandma. I recently got a promo-tion—like yesterday— from cleaning her house to work-ing in the printing business in her garage. She discovered I can spell, so she makes me proofread."

He flashed his killer smile. "So, it's like you're still in school."

"A little. But she said she'd put me to work painting walls as soon as one of her renters moves out."

"Painting walls is fun, but be sure to wear a hat. I forgot one time when I was painting a ceiling, and I ended up with white paint specks in my hair for about a week."

"I'll remember that. I'd hate to look like I was turning gray before my time."

"What color is your hair, anyway? Blonde or brown?"

"They call it dirty blonde."

"Dirty blonde? You made that up."

"Nope. It's a real thing."

"No way."

"Yes, way."

"Well, it doesn't look dirty."

I looked down at my toes with a big, sappy smile on my face, and felt my cheeks go red as his compliment hung in the air. Talking to him, I'd forgotten my period, my unfortunate neckline, and the giant zit on my nose, especially after I noticed that he also had a sprinkling of small zits across his forehead. You wouldn't have noticed if you weren't looking, but I was. He was such a fox. One day, when I was normal, I hoped he would like me.

I was almost sad when Wendy came over.

She floated down onto Susan's towel. Her swimsuit had a green alligator over the left breast. I would have killed for an Izod anything. They were so in style.

Over her shoulder, I saw Lori and the other cheerleaders being chewed out by the lifeguard for jumping on the boys' heads and holding them underwater. Wendy had been in the mix. I didn't know how she escaped the lifeguard's notice. Talent, I guess.

She reclined on the towel. The difference in our tans and shaving success was made clear when she stretched her shapely legs next to mine. I tucked my legs up, embarrassed by the contrast. The scab from my shaving accident had fallen off, but there was still an obvious pink patch.

Funny, I hadn't thought about my legs until she showed up. Another talent of hers, I supposed.

She propped herself up on her elbows and stretched her neck back, trying to make her chest look bigger. That was one thing I had on her, but I wasn't exactly happy about it. Boobs brought too much unwanted attention.

"Good summer, Guinie?" She kept an eye on her foot soldiers in the pool, taking a dunking for their dunking.

"Good, so far."

"How's pom?" She snorted like she knew it couldn't be good.

"It's great!" I seethed through my rubber-band-clenched teeth, but I felt the sting she meant to inflict. I knew pom wasn't as good as cheerleading, but it was nothing to be made fun of. "Coach Jamey is terrific. She used to be a cheerleader at the high school, so she knows what she's doing."

"I know. She was on the varsity squad with my cousin. But Guinie, I feel so bad for you. There are so many losers on pom. Charity Louise? Seriously?! When I learned she was trying out for cheer, I told my mom she absolutely could not make it. She doesn't fit. Can't you just imagine her forgetting to yell, 'Go Panthers,' and yelling, 'Go Jesus,' instead?"

Matt and I laughed, partly because of the way Wendy said it, but mainly because it seemed possible.

The idea of Wendy telling her mom who couldn't be a cheerleader, made me uncomfortable, though. Only two people failed to make the squad, and one of them was me.

Encouraged by our laughter, Wendy kept going. "And be sure to wash your hands if you touch Tonya's pom-poms. Who knows what else she's been groping?" She mimed what Tonya might have had her hands around, and even Matt looked embarrassed.

It was dirty, but kind of funny too, in a shocking way. And now that I'd started laughing, it was hard to stop. It took me a second to realize what she was saying as she tore down my squad.

"And what is Susan wearing? And Jerica? Thank God we don't have any fat cheerleaders, or..."

She stopped talking when something blocked the sun. Correction: when someone blocked the sun. It was Susan. Denise stood a little behind her, shivering even though it was about ninety degrees outside.

"Or Black ones? Or Indians? Is that what you were going to say?" asked Susan.

"Why hello, Susan." Wendy smiled, cool as a cucumber.

"You're on my towel. Get the hell off."

"Language," Denise said, but you could tell her heart wasn't in it.

The lifeguard had stopped lecturing the cheerleaders, so Wendy stood up. "Come on, Matt, let's swim. You coming, Guinie?"

"No," I whispered.

Matt let himself be led away, probably to escape the tense atmosphere that was brewing around me and Susan. He looked over his shoulder at me and made a sad clown face. I guess it was his way of saying, "Sorry, I know you're in a tough spot." It was nice, but it would have been better if he'd stayed around to create a buffer between me and the angry sadness radiating from Susan.

She and Denise sat on their towels. They were silent. Unbearably so. I wasn't sure how much they'd heard, but when I glanced over at Susan, I knew she'd heard it all. She stared straight ahead at the pool, but her eyes looked past it at something I couldn't see. Tears clustered on her dark eyelashes.

"Susan, I never...I wasn't laughing at you. What she said about Tonya was funny and—"

"And what she said about Charity Louise. And Jerica. Wendy's just so funny!" She mimicked me. It hurt, but I deserved it. "It's mean...Guinie," she said with a high-pitched drawl.

When she snapped out the nickname Wendy had given me, I heard how ridiculous it was. I'd never liked it, but now I hated it.

"I'm so, so sorry."

Denise chewed the end of her ponytail, avoiding my eyes.

"Why do you like her?" Susan said, low and serious.

"Who? Wendy?"

"Who else?"

"Well, she helps me. She helped me with cheer."

"But you didn't make it."

"That was my fault."

"You sure? You heard what she said about Charity Louise. Maybe she told her mom—"

"No! She wouldn't do that." But I'd just been thinking the same thing, hadn't I?

"She's a bitch."

For once, Denise didn't remind her about her language.

I'd be lying if I didn't admit Wendy was a bitch sometimes. I'd seen it, but it wasn't all she was. "She can be nice too."

"Especially when you do her homework for her," Denise whispered in a sing-song voice.

"What? You do her homework? You're hopeless, Guinevere."

I knew Susan would take that attitude. It's why I hadn't told her in the first place.

She shook her head when I didn't answer, like she was trying to shake me out of it. "I'm babysitting tonight. Are you ready to go, Denise?"

"Yeah. I guess."

When they left, Denise turned around and put her hand to her ear, telling me to call her later.

I sat there a while longer, hugging my knees and my guilt close to my chest. Susan would never understand why I needed Wendy, the all-powerful. Without Wendy, I wouldn't escape my lousy existence. I'd always be the weird outsider, looking in at the lives of normal families. I wanted to tell Susan and Denise that I liked Wendy because she represented an opportunity for all three of us. That once I made it, I would bring them along with me because I would never, ever leave them behind. They were my best friends forever.

Wendy stood in the still center of the pool, a fixed point in a perfect circle of blue with every person radiating from her. When she pointed, the motion of the pool ebbed and flowed, frothing and waving at her command in an orchestrated water ballet. I half expected her to rise from the foam, like the mighty Aphrodite, perfect and powerful. But Wendy was those already. Everybody knew it. Everybody except Susan.

Then, the goddess reached over and pushed Matt's head under the water. The dunking war began again.

Matt didn't notice when I left the pool and walked home.

Chapter 10

They Say Bad Things Come in Threes

As if I didn't feel wretched enough, as I trudged up The Hill of Infinity, Mrs. Smith's mangy toy poodle, Sweetums, charged at me, attacking my heels in a more vicious than usual assault. The beast was always high strung, but this was an onslaught like no other. Maybe she felt threatened by the flip and flop of my thongs. Or maybe she sensed I deserved it.

"Get off! Go away, you stupid mutt!" I yelled at Sweetums, playing tug-of-war as I tried to keep the thong on my foot.

Sweetums had hooked her sharp little teeth into the purple plastic and pulled for all she was worth. The tiny dog was stronger than she looked.

I yanked and found myself standing with a bare foot while Sweetums retreated a few steps. She stood over my sandal while she bared her tiny, lethal teeth and repulsive, black-speckled gums. Her snarl dared me to retrieve my footwear.

I did not dare.

Mrs. Smith, who had been working in her flower bed, was drawn by the sound of her precious dog's menacing yaps. She came running, one fist in the air and the other waving her pointed garden shovel. The old lady ran faster than you'd think possible.

She snarled too, and I swear her gums were as repulsive as her dog's. Her false teeth wiggled around on them, threatening to eject from her mouth to attack me of their own accord.

"You kids! You hooligans! Kicking my Sweetums! Tearing up my yard!"

"I wasn't kicking her. She attacked me. Took my thong."

"Kids! Hooligans! Good-for-nothings!" She scooped up her rat dog, who had a firm hold on my sandal.

"Mrs. Smith!" I yelled, afraid to step on her lawn lest she unleash the beast. "Mrs. Smith!" I shouted in case she didn't have her hearing aid in. "Can I have my shoe? Please?"

I ended up limping home with one bare foot. I'd have to take seventy-five cents from my savings and go to TG&Y to buy a new pair of thongs. Dumb dog. I considered borrowing Susan's German Shepherd, Killer, and introducing him to Sweetums. It would have been unfair to Killer, though. Sweetums would eat him for lunch.

Then I remembered that I couldn't introduce Killer to Sweetums because Susan probably wouldn't talk to me until we were as old as Mrs. Smith.

And nobody would blame her, not even me.

At the top of the hill, by the Catholic church, was a big patch of clover humming with bees. It would serve me right to get stung by a bee as punishment. Maybe that's why Sweetums took my shoe: as a judgment from God, divine retribution. I halfway thought about stopping in to ask the priest, because he would know, but I didn't because I'd only met him once, back when Mom was thinking about becoming a Catholic.

I deserved to be judged, but even so, I walked on the hot asphalt instead of the soft clover because bee stings hurt.

For the first time in forever, Mom had given me the key to the house. She said I could change clothes, feed the pets, and clean the litter box, but then I had to report to

Mamaw's. I was not to stay at home by myself. And under no circumstances could I burn the house down. She would find out.

I heard the phone ringing through the front door. I unlocked it and rushed in so fast that Merlin swiped air instead of my head. I hoped and prayed it was Susan. Even if she chewed me out and told me I was lower than doggy-doo, it would give me a chance to apologize again. To explain.

I tripped over Morgan le Fay on the way to the phone. She had a habit of falling asleep in any inconvenient place when the mood struck her. For the second time in one day, I was barked at by a vicious old dog. Morgan's asthmatic bark set the budgies twittering.

Finally, I reached the hall, scooped up the handset, and breathlessly said, "MacKenzie residence."

"Fawn?"

"Hey, Dad. It's Guinevere."

"Wow! You sound like your mom, clenched teeth and all." He laughed.

"Oh, that's my rubber bands. Just a minute." I unhooked the bands and dropped them in the little trash can in the bathroom. "Yuck. Orthodontia. Is this better?"

"Much friendlier. It's noisy there."

Morgan barked, the budgies twittered, and Winston and Clementine repeated their "Beam me up" nonsense.

"It's always noisy here. Mom's menagerie." I took the phone into my room and shut the door. "Better?"

"Yes. So, how are you doing, kiddo?"

How to start? It's amazing how, in the space of a breath, a million ideas can flash through your mind. I could have told him I'd just lost my best friend, but that required a lot of explaining. I could have told him I was a jerk who laughed at my friends, but ditto.

I settled for, "Fine. What time are you picking me up on Friday?"

"Actually, that's why I'm calling. I've...well...I've had a thing come up."

"You're not coming?"

"No, kiddo. Sorry."

"Again?"

He paused. "Now you really sound like your mom."

My vision was all messed up, like I was looking through pool water. I took a ragged breath to keep my voice steady.

"Do you realize it's been exactly nine weeks since the last time I came to your place?"

He paused again. "No. I didn't realize it had been that long."

"And that I haven't seen any of the spring movies because I was waiting to go with you? And now the summer movies are coming out?"

"The summer movies are better."

"That's completely irrelevant, Dad."

"I'm sorry, Guinevere. Things have been crazy around here. How about if you come over the weekend after next? It's off schedule, so you'll have to ask your mom."

"Can we go to the movies?"

"Yes. I heard there's a new Mel Brooks movie coming out."

"I looooove Mel Brooks!"

"I knooooow! And Guinevere? Well, I have someone I want you to meet. I think you'll like them."

I groaned. "Another new girlfriend? What's this one into? Meditation? Macrame? Modern Dance?"

He laughed for real, the laugh I liked. The one that sucked me in every time and made me forget he never paid child support and forgot my weekend on the regular.

"No, no! None of that. No more crazy girlfriends. This one's a dental hygienist. Real normal. Real nice."

"I'll believe it when I see it."

"It's true. Ask your mom about that weekend. Love you, kiddo."

He'd said the words, the ones I couldn't stop thinking about. I lay back on my bed while they chased each other through my brain. Normal. Nice. Normal. Nice. Normal. Nice. That's what Dad liked. That's what everyone liked. I was neither.

Other words joined the chase. Hopeless. Crazy. Weird. Mean. Careless. Irresponsible. They got all mixed up inside of me until I shouted, "Stop!"

My plan to make myself normal wasn't going so great, but there was still time. The summer stretched before me.

I pulled the spiral notebook with my list off the bookshelf and drew a thin pencil line through number three: Become best friends with Wendy Walters. She got me into this mess, and Susan was right about her. But still, Wendy was powerful. Could I achieve my goals without her? It required careful thought.

One thing didn't require thought, though. I added it to the list.

11.   *Don't be a jerk.*

Because what's the point of achieving your greatest desire if you lose your friends in the process?

I looked up at the seven Scott Baio's on my wall. I'd added the new pullout poster from *Tiger Beat* to my collage. They all smiled at me with that reassuring smile.

"What now, Scott?"

He seemed to think for a minute, logically deciding which course of action was best. The sunlight from the window glinted off his perfect teeth.

"I'd get a bologna sandwich then take a nap," I said in my best Scott Baio voice.

"Thanks, Scott. Best thing I've heard all day."

I WOKE WITH A start when my bedroom door crashed into my bedroom wall. The pale, hazy light poking my eyeballs told me it was morning. Geesh! I took the longest nap in history. Call the Guinness World Record people.

Merlin jumped on the bed. After a headbutt to my chin, an experimental bite of my nose, and some pointy-clawed kneading of my chest, I wrapped my arm around him and pulled the purring heater close. "You're not allowed in here," I mumbled before closing my eyes again.

"Don't you have pom practice? I can drop you off on my way to work," Mom said.

Groan. I couldn't do it. I knew I was a chicken, but I just couldn't go. The whole squad would know what I did. It would be me against them. Charity Louise would probably call a prayer meeting to intercede for my mean, despicable heart. I just couldn't. *Groan.*

"Do you have practice or not?"

"I can't go."

"Are you sick?"

Another cat pounced on my bed. I didn't move. "Kinda."

"There's no such thing as kinda. You're sick or you're not. Which is it?"

I could have lied, but it seemed like I was in enough trouble. "Not sick."

"Then get up. You're the one who wanted to do pom. If you're going to do something, you need to do it. Leaving in ten."

She slammed my door, leaving the cats behind.

I pulled on a terry cloth romper, brushed my teeth, rolled on deodorant, spritzed on Love's Baby Soft, and was ready to go. Who cared if I was going to see everyone I knew? There was no making a good impression on them. They already hated me.

Imagine my surprise when Jerica ran up to me excitedly to share the good news: Rhonda had joined the pom squad. Our pompom passes were about to become legendary.

"Hey, Guinevere, cute romper," Tonya said as she smothered her lips with Kissing Slicks lip gloss. There was a hickey on her neck.

Charity Louise whispered to me, her voice filled with genuine concern, "Do you think someone choked her?"

"Don't worry," I whispered without a hint of sarcasm about Charity Louise's lack of knowledge, which was probably a first for me. "It's not a bruise. Or at least, not that kind of bruise."

"Oh, good." She still looked worried, though.

"Ready! Let's go, girls," Coach Jamey bubbled.

Everything was so...normal.

I looked over at Susan. She sat, sad and silent, on top of a picnic table. My eyes met hers, and she looked away.

Denise sat next to her, sad and squirmingly uncomfortable, but silent. I fell asleep yesterday before I could call her.

It was abundantly clear to me, though, that they hadn't told the other girls what I'd said.

Boy, oh boy was I a rat, with a capital R. Nothing else in our whole long friendship since kindergarten revealed to me so clearly what amazing friends they were. And I'd thrown it away.

The electronic beat of "Funkytown" blasted from the tinny speakers of Coach Jamey's cassette player.

"Come on, girls, let's teach Rhonda how to pass pompoms." It was maybe the bubbliest I'd ever seen our Coach.

To keep my mind off things, I threw myself into practice, pouring myself into the routine Jamey had choreographed for our first football game halftime show. I "shook it," and pivoted and passed the pompoms with precision.

Old folks walking on the park track stopped to watch us. People in the parking lot let their cars idle as they took in the performance. When practice was finally over, I looked up to see Wendy and her mother watching. They stood in identical, hands-on-hips poses, with identical looks of horror on their faces. Did they think we were terrible or too good? You never could tell with those two.

Rhonda came up to me. "Guinevere, I had no idea you could dance like that. When I got lost, I just followed what you were doing. You've got the stuff."

"Thanks, Rhonda. I'm so glad you joined pom." In the distance, I saw Denise gesturing wildly to Susan as they talked. Denise even stomped her foot.

"Hey-hey-hey," a new voice said, sidling up beside me. "Lookin' good."

The boy only came up to my shoulder, but he was muscley. He had an afro like Willis on *Different Strokes* and wore jeans and a jean jacket. I could tell he wasn't from around here. Everyone from here knows that: jeans + jean jacket + summer + Oklahoma = heatstroke.

"Girl, you dance like The Solid Gold Dancers," he said.

I blushed. "Wow. Thanks."

"Don't listen to him," said Rhonda. "This is my cousin Ronald. He just moved here from Harlem. Thinks he's hot stuff. Come on, Ronald. We've got chores to do."

They walked away arguing in that playful way some families have.

I looked back over at Susan, but she was already halfway down the block. Denise came running over to me.

"Guinevere, are you going to the pool?"

"Shouldn't I go talk to Susan?"

She hung her head. "No. Not now. She's still mad. You know she's sensitive about her weight. Give her time."

"Oh."

"Do you want to swim?"

"You didn't tell the other girls. Thank you."

"Of course we didn't. Friends don't snitch."

I felt a million times worse.

"So, about the pool. You going?"

"I'm sorry, Denise. I've still got my period." Plus, I just didn't feel like it.

"Oh. Shoot. Periods stink."

"They do. I'm sorry." I hugged her and walked home. When I got to the corner, I saw her walking by herself to the pool, carrying her bag on her shoulder.

Chapter 11

Hello again, Hello

Working for Mamaw kept me busy, but guilt and worry gnawed at me, so the next day, I called Denise.

"What should I do? I'm ready to apologize."

"She's not ready to hear it, unless you're willing to stomp Wendy into the mud."

I sighed. I'd marked Wendy off my list, but that wouldn't be enough for Susan.

"You won't do it?"

"Of course, I will." My tone lacked conviction because I was worried. Stomping Wendy was inviting disaster. Better to just gently steer clear.

Denise was silent.

"I'm really sorry. I wasn't laughing at her. I was just laughing. Nervously. I got started and couldn't stop."

"With that attitude, you'll just end up fighting with each other." She groaned, and I could picture her cute little face, all scrunched up. "Hate to say it, but you both need more time."

We hung up.

Luckily, we didn't have pom practice for a few days because Coach was going on vacation to Silver Dollar City with the boy she was pre-engaged to and his family.

I didn't go to the pool because I didn't want to ruin Susan's fun by polluting her space. It was a serious sacrifice because I'd been hoping to see Matt again. Mom wondered why I wasn't using the $25 pass she'd paid for. When I told her it was "that time of the month," she left me alone and went back to studying.

She was taking Organic Chemistry. She said it was hard, and when I glanced at her textbook, I believed her. It was all diagrams of molecules branching out to join other molecules, and math problems that used symbols I'd never seen, even though Principal Duncan let me skip ahead and take Algebra I with the ninth graders last school year. Next year, he was going to let me walk over to the high school to take Geometry.

Mom said she'd rather take an English class or something, but if she was ever going to get a job that paid better than being a file clerk, she needed to take chemistry.

I wondered if Dad's new girlfriend had to take Organic Chemistry to be a dental hygienist. I thought about asking

Mom, except I hadn't told her he had a new girlfriend. I didn't want to make her mood even worse. What with studying, working, and taking care of her animals—and me, of course—she was a grouch day and night.

I tried to help her out as much as she would let me, but that wasn't much. Woe be to the person who cleaned her spaces, making it impossible for her to find all the junk she collected. I kept my room spotless, though. I did my laundry. And I knew how to cook, despite the unfortunate incident with the mac and cheese.

Luckily, we had Mamaw.

She had thought of all kinds of jobs for me, but at the measly rate she paid, it would take the entire summer to pay back the money she had advanced to me for pom. When Grandpa Gerald got home from work each day, he let me do jobs in his woodshop or help cut the grass at the rent houses. He always paid me a little extra, but we had to keep it on the down-low from Mamaw.

To save money, I was sewing my pom squad skirt from a kit. As soon as I looked at the instructions, I understood why it cost less if you sewed it yourself. Sewing in Home Ec didn't prepare me for box pleats. They were like sewing a puzzle. Mamaw helped as much as she could. She was a good seamstress, but Mom was a genius at it. I tried to get her to help, but she said she hadn't wanted me to do pom in the first place, and she didn't have the time. And for goodness' sake, get out of her hair.

On Sunday, I went to the Assembly of God church with Mamaw. I knew I wouldn't run into Susan there because she was a Baptist. I got to wear the red jumper with the white bow blouse that I liked so much.

Because it was only five blocks away, we decided to walk. Mamaw wasn't a big talker unless she had something to complain about, and there was no reason to complain that beautiful morning. The temperature was the coolest it would be all day, and the azaleas were blooming bright. We walked in companionable silence past my old elementary school.

I missed it. Life wasn't perfect back then—not by any stretch of imagination—but it was simpler. Before hormones came on the scene, offering up zits, boobs, boys, and turmoil, I never thought about who I was; I just knew. But after, I didn't know what I thought from one minute to the next about anything, including religion. I liked Mamaw's church, though. I'd been there a bunch. I didn't have my own patch of pew cushion reserved or anything, but I was familiar enough to slip into a comfortable spot when I showed up.

When we walked through the doors, Mamaw's brother and his wife gave me a welcoming hug. They said it was too bad I didn't make it in time for Sunday School, but they were sure the Lord would have a word for me in the main service. They were Sunday School Co-Superintendents, so I'm guessing they were required to say that.

My hand got shook by smiling people so many times between the door and the sanctuary that it was in danger of falling off, but I didn't care. It was a small price to pay for being liked.

The music was great! It was mainly the same old hymns and praise choruses they sang at The Jesus Inn, but accompanied by a grand piano, a Hammond b3 console organ—the kind used by gospel players and blues musicians everywhere—and a pastor in a suit and tie. Plus, everyone wore shoes. Each to their own, but I liked church with shoes on better. Mamaw's church wasn't a free-for-all, and it wasn't swanky like the Episcopalians; it was just normal.

Too bad, Mom didn't like it. It had something to do with being "under her family's thumb," which I halfway understood.

The sermon was good, exciting, but when the pastor said Jesus wanted us to come as we were, I got kind of confused. Here I was trying to remake myself based on a Call of God, and now they were telling me I didn't have to make any changes. I had to admit, though, that I might have misheard that call. And it was equally possible that I had heard what I wanted to hear. I hated those hormones and what they'd done to my brain.

Just like that night at The Jesus Inn, at the end of the service, the pastor invited the weary laden to lay their burdens at the altar. I'd prayed the Prayer of Salvation many times, only to mess up right afterward. In the Lamb's Book of Life up in Heaven, I imagined there was a patch of White Out so thick from putting my name in and whiting it out, that the book wouldn't close all the way. But the guilt I felt about Susan and the other girls was terrible.

While the organs' majestic chords filled the sanctuary, the congregation sang,

"Just as I am, without one plea, but that thy blood was shed for me, and that thou bidd'st me come to thee, O Lamb of God, I come, I come."

I prayed the saving prayer again: "Dear Jesus. Save me from my sins, and please write my name back in the book even though you've had to write it a dozen times at least. Forgive me for being mean to my friends. And please, Lord, help me to stop being a jerk."

I'd faced God, now I had to face Susan—if she'd see me.

I missed my friends. I missed their giggles. I missed their swearing. It was lonelier than the time in third grade when I got head lice, and nobody would sit with me for months afterward except Susan and Denise.

That Thursday, as I sat on the concrete slab that passed for a front porch, re-reading *Seventeen* magazine and making a list of "essential wardrobe items" to look for the next time I went garage sale shopping with Mamaw, I looked up and saw Denise walking down the street.

Denise, as I've mentioned before, was pocket-sized, but that day, she looked a whole foot taller. Her head was up, her fists clenched at her sides. She walked straight up to the porch and stopped, staring me in the eyes.

"Guinevere, get your suit. We're going to the pool."

"Hello to you, too."

"There's no time for that. Let's go."

"Will SHE be there? Does she even want to see me?"

Denise screeched. She may have pulled a few of her hairs out. "I can't take it anymore. I need my friends back. And I want to swim."

"Fine. Give me a minute."

I changed into my swimsuit and threw on a tank top and shorts over it. Unfortunately, I hadn't made it to the store to buy new sandals yet, so I wore my grody old tennis shoes. The remaining bleach-damaged rubber clung desperately to the canvas.

I announced to Mom, "Going to the pool."

She answered, "It's about time."

But halfway there, Denise took a left turn.

"This isn't the way."

"It's a shortcut, by way of Susan's house." She lowered her eyebrows, daring me to refuse her.

I did not dare.

I trudged along after her, the knot in my stomach getting bigger and bigger. "This is pointless. She doesn't want to see me."

Denise turned on me. I stopped in my tracks.

"You're both ridiculous. She's pouting and sad. You're pouting and sad. And I'm stuck in the middle. It's not fair. You started this so you're going to have to suck it up and grovel if you must."

"I'll go, but it won't do any good if she won't listen."

"Convince her. You're the person who persuaded Delmer Dinkins to stop pinching all the girls on the playground. I didn't think anyone could do that."

"Only because I told him if he didn't stop, I'd arrange it so he'd never have children. Ever. I don't think that threat will work for Susan."

"Whatever it takes, do it."

This was a side of Denise I'd never seen. She hadn't giggled once. It made me think she was the one who should do the convincing. Under her orders, I walked up to Susan's door.

Her family lived in the Sunny Acres trailer park. She called it her trailer mansion because her home was made of two double-wides joined by a hallway her dad built. They needed two trailers because her family was big: mom, dad, grandma, Susan, five siblings, and the occasional cousin.

There were about a dozen bikes and kids in the yard, some of them Jacksons, some of them visiting.

Through the screen door, I spied Susan's grandma sitting in her rocker watching TV. It sounded like *General Hospital*, which was a great show. I watched it with Mamaw when she wasn't working my fingers to the bone.

Behind me, Denise hissed, "Knock!"

I knocked.

"Come in, chickees. Come in. Welcome," Susan's grandma said.

Denise went right up and kissed her on the cheek. "Hi, Grandma." Her parents were so old that she didn't have a grandma anymore, so she borrowed Susan's.

Mrs. Jackson was a tiny, wiry lady with deep wrinkles and short salt and pepper hair. I remember Susan telling me, it caused a shock in the family when she whacked off her long hair, but she told them she was too old to care anymore. It was easier to cover short hair with the net she wore when she worked in the elementary school cafeteria.

"Give me a kiss, Guinevere." She tilted her cheek my way.

I gave her a peck. "Hi, Mrs. Jackson."

"Grandma, remember."

"Ok, Grandma." I laughed.

"Let me look at those eyes." She took a good, long look. "Never get tired of those eyes. Greenest green I ever did see."

"Thanks," I said, scooting onto the couch. I pointed to the couple on the TV. "What's going on with Luke and Laura?"

"They're still looking for that diamond. And I think there's going to be a wedding." Grandma's eyes twinkled with excitement.

"Ooh! Really? Like the royal wedding that's coming up."

"Lots of good reasons to get up in the morning," she chuckled.

Denise cleared her throat. She twitched her head toward the back of the trailer like she had a tic. "This is no time for TV. Come on."

"She looks serious," Grandma said. "I'd go if I were you."

I followed Denise down the hall to Susan's room.

Her bedroom door was plastered with handwritten signs: Stay out! Beware! Knock or Die!

Who could blame her? It was universally acknowledged by teenagers everywhere that you could never have enough privacy, and privacy was in short supply in Susan's crowded house.

Denise knocked. "It's me, Suzy-Q."

"Entre," Susan said in the fake, pompous voice I loved.

I stood back when Denise opened the door.

Susan sat on the edge of her unmade bed, using a TV tray as a desk. On it was the drawing book and pad of heavyweight paper I gave her for her birthday. A charcoal pencil was in her hand, a smudge of charcoal on her nose.

Her drawings were taped up all over the brown paneling of her walls, along with a couple of posters of Matt Dillon. He played a jerk in that movie, *The Bodyguard*, but he was such a hunk, you kind of forgot about it.

When I stepped forward, her face went from smiling to scowling in a heartbeat. She turned her back, so she didn't have to look at me.

"You tricked me, Denise. What is she doing here?"

Denise growled like a rabid dog. "Susan Jean Jackson, you are being stupid. *Grr.* And stubborn. *Grr.* And you know it. *Grr. Grr.* I'm telling you the same thing I told Guinevere; I've had it with you two. I need my friends, so you better make up. Or else. *Grr!!!*"

During this impassioned speech, Susan slowly turned around, giving Denise her full attention. She was as in awe of this change in our friend as I was.

"Susan?" My voice shook. I was ready for her to verbally jump on me, but she didn't. She just looked at me, more sad than angry.

I took a breath and dove in.

"I'm going to come right out and say it. I'm sorry. I was stupid and mean, and I made a huge mistake, and if you don't forgive me and give me a chance to do better, I don't know what I'll do because you are my best friend, along with Denise, and nobody will ever replace you."

"You don't think I'm too fat to be on pom?"

"I don't even think you're fat."

"Oh, come off it. I am! I've been on every diet. Cabbage soup, grapefruit, cottage cheese, calorie counting. I bet you don't know how many calories are in a banana. Well, I do. 105. But nothing works."

"So what? You're beautiful and you're fantastic at pom. Wendy's just worried pom will outshine cheer when the football season starts, so she wants to tear us down. I saw her watching us during practice, and she definitely looked worried."

"We're going to crush them," Denise said, grinding her fist into her palm.

It was the first time since that day at the pool that I'd heard her giggle. And even though giggling while grinding her fist was slightly psycho, it was good to see Denise happy again.

"But what about Wendy? Are you still going to be her flunky?" Susan asked.

"Uh! I was never—"

"You were doing her homework!"

"Not all of it. Just select pieces."

"Select pieces? G, she's using you. I don't care how nice you say she can be when she feels like, she's the bitchiest bitch who ever bitched—"

"Language!"

"—and as soon as you're not useful to her, she'll turn on you."

I rolled my eyes, but only a little. Wendy was mean to Susan and the rest of the pom squad, but she could be nice. Giving up on her was like throwing the baby out with the bath water or something, and I didn't think that was part of God's plan for me. I needed to make peace with my friends, though, so I held my tongue and raised my right hand.

"I solemnly swear that I won't be Wendy's flunky, and I won't let her run down my friends and our squad."

"And you won't do her homework anymore," said Susan.

I raised my hand again. "I won't do her homework."

"Good," she stood up and wrapped her arms around me and Denise, "because I need my friends."

"Weirdos forever!" said Denise.

"Weirdos forever!" Susan said with gusto.

I hugged them hard, implying that I agreed. Why did it have to be weirdos, though? Being a weirdo meant struggling like my mom and dad. It destined you for a life tied to someone like Timmy, who was going nowhere, by way of the unemployment office.

Why couldn't we do something different? Something mainstream. Being normal meant going to junior college and being pre-engaged to a nice boy with prospects like Coach Jamey was. I wanted that for all of us: me, Susan, and Denise.

I sighed and hugged them harder. I'd convince them later. Just then, I was glad to be friends again.

"I love you guys. Friends forever!"

Chapter 12
Freezer Pillow

Susan, Denise, and I hung out and talked all day, and never made it to the pool. It was so amazing to have my friends back that I only regretted missing the possibility of seeing Matt a teeny bit. I wouldn't have the chance to see him over the weekend because the next day, Friday, I was going to my dad's. For real. He solemnly swore like I did to Susan, though it was on the phone, so I don't know if he raised his right hand or not.

I was going to meet his new girlfriend, which I wasn't that excited about. I was very excited about going to the new Mel Brooks movie, *History of the World, Part I*. I was also excited because Dad had cable TV and would let me watch anything I wanted, unlike Mamaw and Gerald. I was even a little excited about his goulash, but only for nostalgic reasons. But what had me charged up was that he had air conditioning. If only I could survive the sweltering night, I'd have a chance to enjoy it.

It was still June, but "hot" didn't describe the temperature. Toasty, simmering, roasting, and the rest of those cooking words were inadequate to describe it. I felt like I'd been marinated in vegetable oil and sweat, then popped under the broiler. Even lying on top of the sheets didn't help.

I rolled over on my side to face the screen. The window was open, but only a few puffs of breeze made their way into my room. My face was so sweaty and oily that by the time Dad picked me up, he wouldn't recognize me because I'd be covered in zits. I could feel them under the surface, waiting to pop out.

In the dark outside, the whirr of a solitary cicada started low and climbed to a crescendo before abruptly hitting a rest. Then it began again, but in a chorus. It was a regular cicada opera on the other side of the screen. Too bad I wasn't a fan of opera.

Mom loved the stuff. She had this one record of *Lucia di Lammermoor* that she sang along to when she was feeling down. When she put it on, I made my way to the back of the yard to sit on the old, rusted swing set until her mood passed. Mom's high, dramatic soprano sounded great, but if you knew the plot of the opera, you'd understand why I hightailed it out of there.

I flopped onto my back and rearranged my hair so it hung over the pillow and wouldn't stick to my neck. It was so dark that all I could see of the seven Scott Baios were his pearly whites.

"Sleep tight, Scott."

I wondered if Matt was sleeping tight. With my eyes closed, I pictured the drops of pool water clinging to his eyelashes, to the pale hair on his legs. I imagined reaching out and running my hand over those tanned legs. Imagined him touching me back. Geesh! All that imagining was making me even hotter. I opened my eyes.

Above my dresser was a shelf that Grandpa Gerald hung, and on the shelf were porcelain figurines of Holly Hobbie and her friends, doing fun, wholesome things. I sensed their scorn, shock, and surprise at what I'd been thinking about.

The hum of the oscillating fan in Mom's room made me jealous for half a minute until I remembered that oscillating fans are only good at moving hot air from point A to point B.

The only fan that was any good was an attic fan. They were, without a doubt, the greatest invention ever known for creating an actual breeze as the giant fan sucked in air from outside and pulled it into the attic.

The problem was, the attic fan in our house squeaked and rumbled and coughed something terrible. Mom didn't like to turn it on because it sounded like it was going to fall out of the attic and onto our heads.

I argued with her that a quick death by attic fan, though tragic, was preferable to a slow death by drowning in my sweat as it puddled around me. She said she wouldn't respond to my sarcasm, and besides, she had to work in the morning, and she needed to sleep. Which is why she got custody of the completely pointless oscillating fan.

The glow of the clock on my bedside table read 12:42. If I didn't get to sleep, I knew I'd be grouchy and end up saying something inappropriate to Dad's girlfriend and making a bad impression. And while I didn't care about her, I did care about Dad asking me to come over again.

It was time for drastic action. It was time for Freezer Pillow.

I was always surprised when I met people who had never heard of Freezer Pillow because it was the key to surviving a nuclear apocalypse or a sweltering summer night.

This is how it worked:

1. Sneak out of bed clutching your damp from sweat pillow. Tiptoe down the hall, being careful to step over the threshold of the living room because it squeaks and you do not, under any circumstances, want your mom to wake up and remind you she has to sleep so she can put food on the table because your no-good, lazy dad has not paid child support for the last many years.

2. Open the fridge. Swipe a piece of bologna. Tear off a piece to feed your mom's stupid, noisy cats before they start yowling, thereby waking your mom, who will remind you she needs to sleep. (See #1)

3. Silently open the freezer door with just the right amount of tug so the ice cube trays don't rattle—a maneuver that must be practiced and honed. Briefly stick your entire head into the freezer to enjoy the blast of frigid air.

4. Hold your pillow up to the freezer, blocking the cold so that all of it goes into the pillow. As you wait for the pillow to get frosty, eat the remain-

ing bologna, paying careful attention to the meat that sticks to the red plastic ring, which should be considered bonus bologna.

5. When you begin to feel the cold seeping through the non-freezer-facing side of the pillow, flip the pillow over for maximum freeziness.

6. Silently close the freezer. Creep rapidly back to your room before the pillow loses its frostiness. Avoid stepping on the stupid cat who is always underfoot. Be sure to take the red ring from the bologna with you to hide in your room so your mom can't accuse you of being a bottomless pit of hunger.

7. Lay your head on the icy-cold pillow. Enjoy the way the crisp cotton pillowcase snaps. Revel in the ice crystals that have formed from your former icky sweat. Let the cold envelop and calm your restless brain. It is Heaven. A frozen oasis in a teeming atmosphere of fire.

8. Sleep at last.

Chapter 13

Believe it or Not

FRIDAY EVENING FOUND ME once again sitting on the front step, swatting mosquitoes with my small suitcase beside me. But this time I was 100% positive that he was coming. Which raised the question, if I knew it, why did I have a knot in the pit of my stomach? Luckily, it disappeared when I spotted the lemon-yellow convertible MG Midget driving down my street. It was a British car, which is why Dad bought it; he was obsessed with America's former overlords. Unfortunately, it didn't run any better than Swooshie, but it was more stylish.

He was the only one in it, which was a good thing because it only had two seats. And also, because I still hadn't told Mom about his new girlfriend.

When he pulled into the driveway, convertible top down, I noticed he'd grown a thick brown mustache to match his thick brown hair. Maybe he was trying to look like Magnum P.I. Mom thought the actor was sexy. Maybe Dad's girlfriend did too.

"Ello gov'na!" Dad said, in the worst British accent ever.

"The rain in Spain falls mainly on the plain," I enunciated, as I wedged my suitcase in the sliver of space between the seat and the trunk, or the boot if we're going whole-hog Anglophile.

Mom stepped out on the slab of concrete that passed for a porch. She still wore the pastel blue pants and matching blazer she'd worn to her job sorting and filing mail for a big religious organization. She'd tied a colorful, printed scarf around her neck. Mom was never happy unless she was ruining an outfit by accessorizing it with something weird.

"Make sure she wears her rubber bands," she ordered. "Don't drive too fast. And NO TV SMUT!"

"I'll make sure she wears her rubber bands, Fawn," Dad said, revving the engine that he hadn't turned off when he arrived, probably because he didn't want to get dragged into a conversation about the delinquent child support.

While the engine roared, he moved his mouth, but he wasn't saying anything. I turned my head to laugh into my shoulder. He did not say that he was taking me to a rated R movie and that he had no intention of policing what I watched on cable because he had better things to do.

It was a good trick. I tucked it away for future use.

He took his foot off the gas pedal for a second. "Bye, Fawn."

"Bye, Mom." I waved.

She waved back and went into the house, muttering and slamming the door.

With the wind whipping my hair and the engine rumbling, it was too loud to talk or listen to the radio, so I just smiled. And smiled. And smiled. He'd remembered me. By the time we got to his place, my mouth was numb from smiling because he lived way on the other side of town.

The leather seats of his car were cracked, and the gear shift knob had fallen off and been replaced with a tennis ball, but we still got a lot of looks as we drove because it was cute. What wasn't cute was his apartment. It was a dump. One of those big, cheap, sprawling complexes that looked thirty years old by their first anniversary.

Dad pulled into a space in the parking lot and flipped off the ignition.

"Home, sweet home. I kept your pictures of Shaun Cassidy on the wall in the spare room."

"Shaun Cassidy is so last year. I've moved on—to Scott Baio."

"Chachi, eh? Sounds like a trip to QT for movie magazines is in order."

"Yeah, especially if you'd like to contribute to the cause."

"I think I could do that," he said with a laugh.

The suggestion that I refresh my posters was the most reassuring thing I'd heard in a long time. It meant he was keeping space for me, even with a new girlfriend on the scene.

"So, is the dental hygienist inside?"

"No. At work. They'll be home later. By the way, I need to talk to you about them."

"Are you getting married? Or is she already married? With a dozen kids. Or is she an axe murderer or something, like Lizzie Borden?" I mimed swinging an axe.

"Ha. That might be easier to explain. I'll tell you, but first, get settled, and I'll start dinner."

"Goulash?"

"Right-o, Mate!"

I was relieved to discover the living room looked the same as I remembered. One of his old girlfriends was really into Yoga and decided to get rid of all the furniture and replace it with mats on the floor. It was weird. But it looked like the new woman was OK with the cruddy, brown, imitation suede couch and the massive poster of John Travolta wearing his *Saturday Night Fever* white suit that hung over it. And the framed photograph of Queen Elizabeth II, of course. That was the one thing Dad didn't let the Yoga girlfriend get rid of.

Well, that and his *Pride of Scotland* bagpipe album—and I'm not kidding. He flipped it on and went to the kitchen while I took my suitcase and marched to the spare room to the tune of "Hector the Hero."

The room was a combination storage room and study where Dad kept a bed and an empty drawer for me. And yes, multiple Shaun Cassidy posters smiled down from the walls, along with a couple of Andy Gibb. I'd walk over to the convenience store later to update my selection of pinups and maybe get a suicide slushie while I was at it.

In the kitchen, Dad browned the ground beef in an electric skillet while the elbow noodles bubbled on the stovetop.

"Be a dear and open that can of tomato paste, will you? Opener is in the ceramic jar on the counter. And I've moved the rubbish bin to under the sink."

"Rubbish bin? You know, you're not British, right?"

"But it's such fun to pretend, love."

"Well, long live the Queen then."

He laughed, which was my intent.

"Dad, I've got so much to tell you. About pom squad, mainly. I copied down the football schedule for you. You might want to come watch me. And did you know I'm working for Mamaw, and it's like real work in her print shop, not just kid stuff. And I don't think I told you, but I won the spelling bee again, and—"

"Oh, is that the door? Julian's early. Bollocks. And I didn't tell you. Well, hold onto your hat, Guinevere."

Dad ran from the kitchen. I dumped the tomato paste and a can of water into the ground beef. I heard murmuring whispers in the next room, but no words. While I dashed paprika into the electric skillet, Dad came around the corner, followed by a blonde man with a close-cropped blonde beard and piercing blue eyes.

"Guinevere, I'd like you to meet Julian."

A rigor mortis grin was fixed on my face as I blindly stirred the mess in the skillet around.

With God's help, or not, I'd never had much chance of becoming normal, no matter how hard I tried. But after Julian? After Julian, I had no chance at all.

He wore blue scrubs; the same kind Mom wore for her nursing training.

Through an awkward sequence of events that I can't precisely remember because I was processing the unexpected nature of Dad's newest flame, I found myself sitting at the dining table, which was separated from the kitchen by half a wall, with a plate of goulash in front of me. At least there were no animals and food bowls around my feet.

Dad didn't have pets. Mom collected pets, Dad collected ex-girlfriends.

That was one reason I was polite but stand-offish with Julian—not because he was a man, but because I acted that way with all of Dad's new flames. You didn't want to get too attached because you never knew how long they were going to stick around.

Still, I wasn't sure what to think about Dad dating a man. I'd never known anyone who was gay. I kind of figured it was just something they made up for the movies. It was weird when it was your dad, but then again, having your dad go two and a half whole months without bothering to pick you up on your weekend was even weirder.

My main concern was how this would affect my plan to remake myself into a totally normal, non-weird human being. This was going to be hard to overcome.

Julian seemed nice, though. And Dad seemed happy. For the moment. But he'd been happy with Yoga girl at first, too.

"So, you're going to be in high school this fall," Julian said gently as he passed the bottle of Catalina dressing for the salad. He smiled but didn't overdo it. His teeth were very straight.

"Yeah. Kind of. I'll be a freshman, but at my school, the ninth graders are still in the junior high building."

"Every school does it a little differently, I think."

"Seems that way. What did your school do?" I asked, making polite conversation. The goulash needed salt. I was so surprised when Julian walked in that I must have forgotten to add it.

"At my school, ninth grade was in the same building as the seniors. My town was so small, though, that the kindergarteners were just across the parking lot. Everyone knew each other—the good and the bad."

"I know what that's like. It's hard to become a new person when everyone knows you."

Dad huffed. "Why would you want to become a new person, Guinevere? You're perfect as you are."

Tell that to Mrs. Walters, I thought. But I said, "Thanks," as Dad smiled at Julian, seeking confirmation that he should be awarded Father of the Year.

I rolled my eyes. The things we kids had to deal with. Parents constantly complained about the behavior of the average adolescent, but in my opinion, the behavior of the average person going through a mid-life crisis was a thousand times worse. I knew because I'd read about it in Cosmo.

Meeting someone new is always awkward, especially when the person introducing you really, really wants you to get along. It puts everyone under a lot of pressure, but

Julian did a good job of keeping the conversation going. He told a few funny stories about some of the patients he'd worked on.

Dad laughed too loudly, trying too hard. Julian's stories revealed that going to the dentist brings out the worst in people. I knew it did with me; it made me grouchy. I'd only said a dozen words to Dr. Weisbein, and I'd been seeing him for almost two years. I wouldn't be a dental hygienist unless you paid me at least a million dollars.

"Did you have to take Organic Chemistry to be a Dental Hygienist?"

"No, thank God. I've heard it's a beast."

"My mom's taking it. I looked at her textbook. Brutal."

"But Fawn is a genius," Dad offered.

Oops. Dad's tone of voice made it sound like he thought Julian wasn't. Ten to one, Julian would be gone before Christmas.

"I hear you're very smart," Julian said, with merely a raised eyebrow in Dad's direction. He was good. Maybe he'd be around until Easter.

"Well, I won the spelling bee, if you count that, but most people couldn't care less."

They both laughed and finally, having done justice to the goulash, we called quits on dinner. Julian offered to wash the dishes so Dad and I could have father-daughter time.

I plopped on the couch underneath the poster of John Travolta, the poster that had hung there for a few years, at least. I glanced at John in his three-piece white suit, with his finger pointing to the ceiling, and realized the poster should have been clue number one that Dad liked guys as much as he liked women. Mamaw always said Dad was a fruit loop, but I would never tell her she was right because she'd think the apocalypse had arrived.

Dad switched on the TV and pressed the cable box button for HBO before joining me on the couch.

I pumped my fist. "Yes! I'm going to watch so much TV this weekend. Mom refuses to get cable—"

I stopped what I was going to say, but Mom's voice in my head kept on going, "because your dad doesn't pay child support." I redirected.

"—and Mamaw and Gerald police it like the KGB."

"Watch all you want. And we'll go to the movies tomorrow. A matinee, if that works with your schedule, madam."

"Perfectly." I knew it was because the matinee cost less, but I didn't care. I was glad to be going.

We watched and joked around a little. When Julian finished washing up, he came out and gave Dad a peck on the lips. I looked down at my lap because seeing your dad kiss anyone is every bit as embarrassing as seeing your mom flirt.

"I'm so glad I finally got to meet you, Guinevere," he said. "It's been a long day. Two impacted molars and a decaying bicuspid. I'm going to bed early. Night-night."

"Night." I waved.

As soon as the bedroom door snapped shut, Dad looked at me with excited eyes. "So, what do you think? Nice, huh?"

"Yeah, nice." I nodded and shrugged at the same time. Julian was nice, but it's hard to be gung-ho about someone after less than two hours' acquaintance.

Dad took my lukewarm response the wrong way. He collapsed back on the sofa, leaning his head on the back of it as he looked up at the ceiling. "I should have known. You're around your mother too much. It's because he's a he, isn't it?"

"Dad, don't spaz! I said he was nice. I meant it. He's nice, already. A real gem. It's just that I just met him." And given your history, he probably won't be around long. That part, I didn't say.

"You don't care that I'm dating a man?"

"Well..." Did I care? I cared about the death of my social life if anyone found out, that was for sure. Mrs. Walters would have a cow, right out in public for everyone to see. I also cared about Mamaw finding out and being forced to listen to her go on about it for the rest of my life. But did I care about what Dad did on the 330 days a year I wasn't around?

"No, not really. It just took me by surprise. You've always been into women."

"Still am. Women are great. But so is Julian. I swing both ways."

I forced my eyes not to roll. I should have known. Neither of my parents could make decisions and stick with them. They were always trying things out; going through churches, jobs, and flirtations like they were going out of style, for heaven's sake. Trying to find themselves, while they left me to my own devices.

I walked across the room to the cable box and switched it to *The Dukes of Hazzard*. It was better than the crap on HBO.

When I plopped back down on the sofa, I hugged the brown tasseled pillow to my chest and pulled a bit of fluff from the hole where the seam was coming apart. I rolled the fluff between my middle finger and thumb until it made a ball.

"What's wrong, Mate?"

"Nothing." I flicked the fluff ball onto the carpet. "It's just..." Hot tears welled in my eyes. I blinked them back. I would not cry. "Why don't you ever think about me?" The tears ran down my cheeks against my will. "I'm trying really, really hard to be a totally ordinary, normal teenager. But everyone is constantly working against me." I sucked in a breath. "Including you!"

Dad sighed and looked at the ceiling again. "So, you don't like Julian. I knew it."

"Dad! I like Julian. He seems cool. But you've got to admit that on a scale of normal things from 1-10, you dating Julian is like a negative one."

"Since when did a daughter of mine—and Fawn's, for feck's sake..."

He shook his head like he thought Mom was the weirdest person in the world. It made me mad because that was my job.

"...start worrying about being normal?"

"Since I looked around and saw how other people live. I have eyes, you know. Since I got sick to death of being a weirdo."

Dad walked across the room to the cable box and switched the TV back to HBO. "There's a great horror movie coming on. You should see it."

"My life is a horror movie." I pulled another bit of fluff from the pillow.

By the time he sat down again, he was calm. He gently rescued the pillow before I removed all the fluff. He nudged his shoulder against mine.

"What's your definition of normal?" He asked. "What are you aiming for?"

"I want…"

What was I aiming for? Put on the spot, I couldn't put it into words. All I knew was that I wanted a life more like other people had—steady and predictable—and less like the one I inhabited. I was sick of the chaos of my life, with the chaos and weirdness inside me, and wanted to try something else, be someone else. But the words were mixed up inside me, and I couldn't puzzle them into a logical order. Incomprehensible sludge gushed out.

"Normal is just, you know, being able to fit in with everyone. Like, having the same clothes and doing the same things, and stuff. And like, well, you know, having your parents come to the football games and talk to the other parents and stuff, because everyone is friends and their kids are friends. And maybe like, not driving cars that break down and stuff like that."

"Ah, you're talking about middle-class morality kind of stuff."

"I don't think that's what I'm talking about. I don't even know what that is."

"It means having proper behavior and proper attitudes. Living by a kind of code set down by the middle class." He put proper in air quotes.

"Proper seems good."

He put his arm around me and pulled me into a side hug. "It is, until you realize how limiting it is. How much it excludes. It's hard to have middle-class morality when you're not middle class. And we're not, Guinevere. Not even close."

"I can try, though."

We sat without speaking, listening to the ominous music coming from the TV, where a car drove up to some old hotel in the mountains. I was already scared, and the movie was just beginning. I hated horror movies.

"There's no such thing as normal," Dad whispered.

He was so, so wrong. I knew it because I saw it every day.

"I'm calling it a night. We'll have a good day tomorrow. Mel Brooks, right?"

"Right." I smiled. "I love Mel Brooks."

"Goodnight. Enjoy *The Shining*. It's a masterpiece of filmmaking." He squeezed my shoulder before he got up.

"Dad."

He turned back and, framed by the popcorn plastered walls, intoned, "You called?"

I laughed. "Julian is super nice. I like him."

"Thanks, Mate."

When the door to his bedroom clicked shut, I walked across the room to the cable box and pushed buttons until I found something I liked.

As I watched Perry Mason restore order in black and white, I decided: I would love the weirdos in my life—and love them fiercely—but I didn't have to be like them. One day soon, I would be normal, even if drastic action was required.

Chapter 14

My Lips Are Sealed Because These are the Best of Times

THE REST OF THE summer passed in a blur that ranged from mildly interesting to comatose with boredom.

Mom ended her totally-unneeded-and-unnecessary ban on me staying home alone, partly because it was summer and she didn't want to pay for camp, but mainly because she was tired of hauling me around with her and getting no time to herself. She had added doing nurse training at the hospital to working at her office job and taking Organic Chemistry, so I could understand her desire for "me time." I needed it too.

I used my time alone to watch all the TV shows I needed to watch for my research into the normal lifestyle of the

American teen, without Mom huffing and moaning that it was brainless drivel. It involved a lot of *The Facts of Life*, but also a good amount of soap operas because I liked them.

I also kept up with international events, like when I got up at three in the morning to watch Lady Di marry Prince Charles. I had read all the magazine articles about them, and for a while, I thought I'd give up being normal and go straight to being royal. But eventually, I figured out that becoming the first person in my family to achieve total normality was easier.

Not that it was easy. I worked through my list, focusing on remaking my wardrobe. It was only possible because I was still working for Mamaw.

I'd been promoted to typing on the enormous, computerized typesetter she'd brought into her printing business. The thing was bigger than Dad's car, though the keyboard was normal-sized. Choosing typing as an elective in eighth grade turned out to be a great decision; I was fast and accurate. Because of the penny-pinching hourly rate I earned, my typing proficiency worked against me some, but I loved hearing the rapid-fire *clack-clack-clack* of the keys. And I loved it when Mamaw pulled Gerald in from the woodshop one day so he could watch my fingers fly.

He was so proud that he passed me a dollar when Mamaw wasn't looking.

"With typing like that and your good spelling, you're sure to get a good secretary job after you graduate."

That took the wind from my sails. I didn't know what I wanted to be, but after talking to Coach Jamey about college, being a secretary wasn't top of the list. Still, it was a relief to know that if whatever I eventually decided on didn't work out, I'd have typing and spelling to fall back on.

And to think, I'd almost let Susan talk me into taking art with her instead of typing.

One Saturday, with my hard-earned cash in the pocket of my cutoffs, a supply of snickerdoodle cookies in a Tupperware container for sustenance, and Roy Clark pickin' and grinnin' through the truck's speakers, Mamaw and I drove around looking for garage sale signs. Not only was bargain hunting a sport for Mamaw, but she also approved of my mission to improve my appearance. Her good angel and bad angel didn't even have to fight it out because at the end of the shopping day, I'd look more like the other girls, and I'd do it on the cheap.

At those rich houses on the other side of the river, I found some outfits that looked just like the ones in the latest issue of *Seventeen* magazine. And once we got home, full of snickerdoodles and out of cash, Mamaw let me use her sewing machine to alter the clothes that didn't quite fit.

Other than that, I spent the last weeks of summer at pom practice, the pool, and the library. I must have read about 100 books, maybe more. Charlene, the librarian, kept trying to give me books about strong women. They were OK, but I was mainly interested in reading every book in the teen romance section. If I aspired to be a normal teen girl, I figured I should read like one. And besides, those romances weren't half bad.

I had time to read because Susan went to the lake with four generations of her family. Denise went to Dog Patch USA with hers. Matt spent a couple of weeks working on his grandparents' farm. And in between her cheerleading camp, family vacation, and who knew what else, I hadn't seen Wendy in weeks.

Even Mamaw and Gerald went on vacation with friends from their square-dancing group. I hinted that I wouldn't mind going with them. Mamaw said they loved me, but sometimes they needed to do things on their own.

Late in the summer, a new channel started up on cable: MTV. Everyone was obsessed with it, and I was desperate to watch. Mamaw and Gerald thought it was straight from the devil, though, and Mom refused to give up buying groceries and gas for the car just so I could rot my brain with more television. Dad was my only hope. Unfortunately, he'd had a bunch of stuff going on and hadn't been able to pick me up after that one weekend. I called him up anyway to see if I could come over to watch MTV at his place.

"How's Julian?"

"Good...OK...Actually...We had a fight. We'll make up, though."

"I'm sorry." And I was. I wanted Dad to be happy. "I suppose that means it's not a good weekend for me to come over."

"Sorry, Mate, but it's not."

"OK. I hope it works out. I can't believe I'm admitting this, but Julian is the most normal person you've ever dated."

Dad laughed.

I sighed. It was true. And they were doomed.

After I talked to him, I lay back on my bed and looked at my collection of Scott Baio posters. There were eight of them now. I'd scored a new one from Denise, who brought it back for me from her vacation.

"Tell me, Scott. What would you do if your parents were so weird, they sabotaged your chances of reaching your goals?"

Scott one through eight smiled their perfect smiles. They didn't have to worry about not meeting their goals. Scott was successful. He was on TV, for goodness' sake. And he was hanging right there on my wall, eight times. Talk about success. Scott obviously hadn't let a little thing like having parents who wandered off the beaten path stand in his way.

I'd do the same.

One day, at the end of pom practice, the other girls rushed away to swim for a while before the pool closed for the day. I didn't go with them. The day before, I had taken Tonya's advice to use baby oil on my skin in a last-ditch effort to turn my ghostly skin beige before school started. It was too late in the summer for tan. But what I'd succeeded in doing was turning myself a flaming, blistering red.

It was the last time I listened to Tonya.

"You're not going with the others?" Coach Jamey asked.

"No. I think my skin's had all the sun it can stand."

"Wise decision."

"Do you need help carrying that stuff to your car?"

"Actually, if your skin can take it, I'd love your help with our next routine. "Funkytown" looks great, but we can't do it all season."

"It's shady under the trees. I'd be happy to help."

I phrased it like I was doing her a favor, but really, if I'd known a sunburn would give me the chance to work on choreography, I would have gotten one earlier.

"Great! I have a tape of the song I was thinking of."

She popped a cassette into her portable tape player and the beat of Billy Joel's "It's Still Rock and Roll to Me" galloped into the park.

There was something vaguely mathematical about pom that I liked: shapes, points, symmetry, and all that. There was even graph paper to map out the routine, which made me like Jamey even more.

While we danced and graphed out the moves, I listened to her talk about her college classes and her plan to transfer to Oklahoma University in Norman when she finished at the junior college. If she didn't get married first.

The only people I knew who had gone to college were my grandma on my dad's side, who had gone as an adult, and my mom, who was an adult. And my teachers, I supposed. I never talked to them about it. Nobody wanted to know about their teachers' personal lives. For all I knew, they lived at school.

Jamey was the first person I knew who went to college while she was still young.

Anyway, by the time we planned out the routine, the pool had closed, and most people had wandered home for dinner. The lifeguards hurried around the edge of the pool, doing all the stuff they had to do before they could leave.

After Jamey pulled her orange Pinto hatchback out of the parking lot, there were only two cars left. The park was so empty as I began the long walk home that I was surprised to see Wendy sitting by herself on top of a picnic table, elbows on knees, chin in hands. She lifted her hand to acknowledge my presence as I passed, and I waved back. I walked a few more steps until I felt an urge come out of nowhere to stop.

When had I ever seen Wendy alone? In all the long years I'd known her, I couldn't think of one time.

I'd been trying to regain Susan's trust and keep my promise not to be Wendy's flunky, so I hadn't hung out with her since that awful first day at the pool. Honestly, it hadn't been too hard to stay away since Wendy had been out of town. But something about the way she was sitting there tugged at me. I took a chance, turned around, and walked over to her.

"Hey, Guinie." Her voice was deflated, like a balloon with a slow leak.

"What's up, Doc?"

"Not much." Her eyes flicked to her house.

"I've seen some of your practices," she continued, "Pom looks good. Better than I expected. Especially you."

Color me flabbergasted. Deflated Wendy sounded totally honest. She thought I was good. And of course, being unaccustomed to hearing that I was good at anything you can't learn from a school textbook, I made a joke about it.

"Must be because I finally stopped tripping over my own pompoms."

She laughed.

"I haven't seen cheerleading practice, but I know it's great without seeing it. It always is."

She glowed.

"Looking forward to freshman year?" I asked.

"Surprisingly, yes. It will be fun to be the oldest kids at school."

"Yeah, for one brief and shining moment before we start over again at the high school and become shrimps again. Practice for life, I guess. All the adults I know are grunts."

"Maybe that's why my mom keeps saying 'these years are the best years of your life.'" She sounded scarily like her mother.

"Not gonna lie, if junior high is the best years of my life, I'm in trouble."

"I don't know, it seems pretty good to me. On the whole." Her eyes flicked to her house again. "And this year, we'll be Queen Bees. We'll rule over those seventh and eigth graders."

"With an iron fist!" I raised my fist to bring home the thought.

Wendy's eyes sparked with pleasure before fading again. "That will be awesome! Not looking forward to the rest of it, though. Why do we have to learn all that boring junk? We'll never use it."

Being someone who liked most of the boring junk, I'd learned to keep it to myself. Trying to convince people the junk is actually fascinating was no way to win friends and influence people.

I shrugged.

"If it weren't for you, I would have missed cheer camp to go to summer school. Mom would have died from shame. I never really thanked you for that."

Technically, she didn't thank me then and there either, but I got what she was going for.

She took out her ponytail band, then put it back in. "You wouldn't consider helping me again, would you?" Her question hung in the air, demanding an answer.

I pictured Susan, remembered my promise. I also remembered what Susan said about Wendy dropping me if I wasn't useful to her. How miserable would ninth grade be with Wendy against me? Maybe I could make them both happy.

"I could tutor you if you need it. Help you understand the material."

She was quiet for a minute, likely doing the same kind of calculus I'd been doing, studying all the angles.

"That would be great. Thanks."

The front door of her house swung open with a bang. Wendy's older brother came storming out, followed by her dad with a belt in his hand. He whipped the belt in the air like a lion tamer. His pants sagged around his hips.

"No! Don't!" Mrs. Walters cried out as she followed him, reaching for the belt.

The brother slammed the door of his flashy Camaro. The bumper was crushed. He peeled out of the driveway like a bat out of Hell. Mrs. Walters took her husband's arm and dragged him back into the house. She looked around to see if anyone was watching. There were a lot of trees between her and the picnic table, so she probably didn't see me. I hoped she didn't.

Wendy was rigid beside me. She managed to speak without moving her lips. "Don't tell anyone."

"I won't. Who would I tell?"

"The pom girls. Everyone."

"I wouldn't do that. I promise." I remembered what Denise said to me one day, but was Wendy my friend? I hoped so. "Friends don't snitch on friends."

She relaxed, leaned her shoulder against mine. "Thanks. We're not usually like that. We're nice."

And I knew she was talking about her family.

"Of course, you're nice."

By which I meant her family.

"Every family has rough spots," I continued. "Yours is better than mine. At least your parents gave you a normal name. I can never find a key chain with my name on it, but I'd bet you find your name all the time."

"Yeah, Guinevere is a weird name. Did your parents just make it up or something?"

I raised my eyebrow but tried to be gentle. I truly was trying to follow number eleven on my list and be less of a jerk. "Well, no. It's after Queen Guinevere."

It was Wendy's turn to raise an eyebrow. She shrugged.

"You know. King Arthur, Camelot, Lancelot, Morgan le Fay—and Guinevere, Arthur's wife."

"Never heard of it."

"There's a brand-new movie about it. *Excalibur*. Sold a lot of tickets."

"They named you after a movie that just came out?! How is that even possible?"

"Never mind. I'm thinking about changing it. My name, that is."

"What to?"

"I have ideas. I'll let you know when I decide. If I decide."

"Sounds good. Hey, I should probably go home. See what's up."

"Understand."

Before she'd gone far, she turned around. "Hey, Guinie. Friends?"

"Yeah, definitely!" I sat up a little straighter. "Friends."

I'd crossed out number three on my Normal List, but somehow, I'd achieved it anyway. I was friends with Wendy Walters.

I walked up The Hill with a bounce in my step, my mind full of thoughts about what Dad called middle-class morality, college, the hand of God, Billy Joel, our stellar pom choreography, and how even normal families have cracks in them.

The good, the bad, and the confusing.

The only thing I knew for sure was that not even liver and onions could sour my mood.

Chapter 15

New and Improved Guinevere

One and a half weeks later, freshman year began. Same building, same people, new and improved Guinevere Mackenzie. Once I introduced the student body to the new me, they'd be so dazzled, they'd forget about the old, weird me.

How many ways was it going to be great? Let me count them.

For the first time in two years, I could open my mouth all the way because Dr. Weisbein said I didn't need to wear rubber bands anymore. And even better, he said he'd remove my braces by the end of 1981.

For once, my hair curled instead of frizzing.

The pom squad elected me captain, though they flatly refused my suggestion to wear matching shirts on the first day. Jerica spoke for the group when she said it was the lamest-ass idea she'd heard come from my mouth, and that was saying something.

Never daunted, I decided to wear my pride and joy: a real Izod shirt I found at a garage sale at an honest-to-God mansion; the greatest garage sale triumph ever. Every time I looked over the popped collar and saw the little green alligator on the pale pink shirt, I smiled. Who knew I was so fond of reptiles?

At the same sale, I found a pair of tan pleated pants. They were too short, so I hemmed them into a cute pair of knee-length walking shorts. With knee-high socks and a pair of boat shoes from JCPenney, I looked just like the girls in the teen magazines. Except that the shoes looked like shiny, brown plastic instead of leather. I scuffed them up, so they'd look like I'd been sailing before I decided to show up for school.

And best of all, Mom said she could drop me off so I wouldn't muss my ensemble by walking all that way.

"Can you drop me off around the corner?"

"I can take you closer. I have plenty of time," Mom said as Swooshie chugged out a plume of smoke. "My first class isn't until 9:30. I'd hate for that alligator on your shirt to get sweaty."

"Sarcasm doesn't become you. Around the corner is fine."

She rolled her eyes but pulled around the corner from the school. "Have a good day. Don't let the jerks get you down." When she drove away, the car rattled.

From a block away, the front lawn of the school looked like it was swarming with a million ants in constant motion as they competed for resources. But as you got closer, you could see that it was actually a swarm of adolescents in constant motion, competing for resources. Junior high was just like *Wild Kingdom*.

I imagined Marlin Perkins' voice, narrating the scene:

> "The social behavior of the adolescent is dependent on rapidly evolving and devolving groups. They stand in circles facing each other, but every second, a person peels away to join a different group and then another before coming back to the original group. As a result, all groups are left in a state of upheaval."

That Marlin Perkins sure knew his animals.

There were some people standing solo, though, like the new seventh graders who stood like quivering peonies, fearful that the ants would swarm all over them. And then there were the people who hated school, everyone in it, and wanted to be left alone, like Daria Watson, who hadn't smiled in seven years.

Susan and Denise were waiting for me at the corner.

"We're going to rule the school, bitches," Susan said, holding up her hands for a double high five.

"Language…Oh, never mind."

I slapped Susan's hands. "Let's do this!"

We strutted our stuff up the front sidewalk. Jerica, Rhonda, and Ronald joined us, as did Tonya and Charity Louise. We were a pack. And we were cool.

I imagined what we looked like, the Vaseline haze of the shot, the bass pumping as we slow-walked. I flipped my hair, held back by a pink grosgrain headband. On my right, Susan peeked over her sunglasses. On my left, Denise licked her lips, coated with Strawberry Swirl gloss. If the rest of our squad looked half as awesome—and I was sure they did—West Junior High was due for a massive restructuring of the social order, with pom on top.

Splat!

"Ugh!"

When the cherry red slushie landed at my feet, I stopped so suddenly that our pack bumped into each other until we became an undignified cluster. My knee socks were spattered with pink.

"Sorry, Guinevere. It slipped." Horror filled Delmer Dinkins' eyes. His hand moved to protect his baby-making parts.

"Why, Delmer? Why? It's eight in the morning. This is not the time for slushies."

"But they're delicious any time of day. Here, I have a napkin."

I looked at the limp, crumpled thing. "Paltry. I have spots on my knee socks."

Delmer slunk away.

My glamorous pack disintegrated. Most of them went to ask the janitor if he would let them in early to wash the slushie off their shoes. But I, clutching my schedule, went to find my friend, Wendy.

She was easy to find. The sun shone down, anointing her as she stood at the center of the cheerleaders. She had accomplished with cheer what I couldn't with pom: convince them to wear matching t-shirts. Theirs were blue with white iron-on letters that read Angel Squad on the front, with a halo over the A, and their names on the back. The problem was that a few of the ends-with-y girls had transposed their letters. Their shirts said Angle Squad instead.

I figured it was a dumb mistake made by one and repeated by more because they were determined to follow each other blindly, like those lemmings on *Wild Kingdom*. But who knew? Maybe it was a clever ploy to get extra credit in math.

Wendy's shirt was correct. That's why she was the leader.

Before I could get to her, Matt tapped me on the shoulder. He was wearing new Levi's 501s and was, as always and forevermore, a complete fox.

"Hey, Guinevere. Turning preppy?" He smiled as he took in my outfit.

"Just a smidge," I said with a wink, "but don't tell anyone. Maybe they won't notice."

He laughed. "Same old Guinevere." He seemed happy about it.

I was stopped from telling him that I wasn't the "same old" at all. I was the "new and improved," but one of his football friends demanded his attention.

When I turned back to Wendy, she had a weird expression on her face. I shrugged it off. We were officially friends, and besides the new and improved Guinevere needed her stamp of approval so the rest of the student body would fall in line.

"Hey, Wendy. Your hair looks amazing today. But then, it always does."

"Guinie! How sweet!" The weird look retreated behind her smile, but I still saw a glimmer of it around the eyes. "Cute shirt. Where did you get it?"

She emphasized YOU as she eyed my alligator. As in, "Since when can YOU afford Izod?"

"Mall." I don't know why I lied. The whole pom squad knew about my lucky garage sale find. But somehow, I knew Wendy would use it against me. "I like your matching shirts. Cheer went above and beyond."

"We always do. And they are cute, aren't they? Even though some people…" she glared at the angle squad, "had problems with the letters."

"I tried to get the Pomsters to wear matching shirts, but it didn't work out."

"Well, it's a cheer thing, isn't it?"

My head automatically began to nod, a reflex action I didn't understand, but I stopped it. Hold on a minute. Backup. Since when did cheerleaders have the sole right to wear matching shirts? A compulsion to stake my squad's claim to be matchy-matchy if we so desired overwhelmed me.

"It will be fun on Friday when we all wear our uniforms to school for the pep rally, won't it?" I said with teasing innocence as I tried to rub it in her face that we could all match if we wanted.

Her eyes widened ever so slightly before she looked down at her pink painted nails. Her voice was relaxed, off-hand. "Pom's wearing their uniform on game day?"

"Of course. We're doing a preview of our half-time show."

For a millennium, pep rallies had been the domain of the cheerleaders, but there was a new squad in town.

"Oh, how nice."

All who stood near shivered like a polar vortex had vor-texed through.

A change of subject was required before West Junior High's version of the Cold War broke out.

"What classes do you have?"

The pause in conversation as we compared schedules made me realize I'd gotten riled up; I could still feel the blood pumping in my ears. I remembered number eleven on my list. The new and improved Guinevere was not a jerk.

I took a breath and sincerely said, "No classes together. That's too bad. Remember, if you need help, I'm happy to tutor you. And there's always lunch."

"Yeah, lunch," she said as she continued studying my schedule. "You're an aide to the English teacher."

"Uh-huh. They're letting me be an aid so I can leave early to walk over to the high school for Geometry." The high school building was next door, but it took more than the five-minute passing period to get there.

The temperature around us warmed about twenty degrees. "How fun. Will you get to grade papers?"

"Maybe."

"I bet you'll get to put grades in the grade book."

"It's the first day. I don't know yet."

"Too bad you're not the math teacher's aide." She winked.

Uh-oh! I had made a solemn vow that I would not do Wendy's homework. I was pretty sure that other ways of cheating were also included in the agreement. Luckily, I was saved by the bell.

The mass of students surged toward the doors, like they were eager to get to class. By tomorrow, I knew it would be a different story.

"Bye-bye." Wendy waved with her index finger and led the cheerleaders inside.

"See you at lunch." I wasn't sure if she heard me because she was hugging her mother, who stood by the front steps with the other PTA moms.

By lunchtime, I was so hungry that nothing could put me off eating, not even the miasma of odors wafting into the hall: the vomit smell of broccoli cooked until it turned yellow, bleach from the cleaning bucket, and the weird milk smell from the vat where we poured our unfinished milk before tossing the cartons. Steam emitted from the industrial-sized dishwasher as it washed a never-ending line of molded plates, cooking the scents into a barf-inducing stew. Add a pinch of ninth-grade boy sweat and a spritz of Wind Song perfume, and the product was something that stayed on your mind because it clung to your clothes the rest of the day.

I was late arriving on account of having to walk back from the high school building. Being able to work ahead in math was awesome, but I wished I could do it in my own building so I wouldn't be late to the most important social event of the junior high day: lunch.

The cafeteria had all the usual features: rows of rectangular tables, rectangular orange trays to carry rectangular plates with rectangular sections molded in. Quadrilaterals ruled in the cafeteria. Even the pizza had four sides, four angles, and four vertices.

One thing our cafeteria had going for it was light. Long rows of rectangular windows looked over the sports fields on one side and the teacher's parking lot on the other. Since most of the classrooms only had small windows near the ceiling, it was nice to soak up the sun while catching up with your friends over a plate of mystery meat. It made you feel human.

Since I was late, I sailed through the line in record time.

Wendy was at her usual table in the center of the cafeteria. She had claimed it on the first day of seventh grade, and two years later, there was still nobody brave—or stupid—enough to challenge her for it. I always wondered why she hadn't staked a claim at a table next to the windows. Susan said it was because Wendy wanted to be the center of attention in our hearts and eyes, but that was a cynical way of looking at things if you asked me.

Unfortunately, she hadn't saved a seat for me despite our morning conversation.

Every table in the cafeteria was full. Everyone sat where they'd sat the last two years.

Was I the only one in the whole history of junior high with an itch to switch? Nobody warns you that the table you pick as a measly seventh grader is your table for life. Somebody should write a guidebook for the junior-high babies. Or even better, do away with the whole dumb system.

Though it did make it easy to find Susan even without her arm waving like an oil-pump jack. The Pomsters had saved a seat for me next to the window. Our designated end of the table was nearly 200% fuller this year. It was the only section in the cafeteria to show a material change in its composition.

I squeezed between Susan and Jerica. Rhonda, Tonya, and Charity Louise were opposite, spread out to save a spot for Denise. She was usually late because she had to go to the office for her hyperactive meds.

"Is that all you're eating?" I asked Susan. She had a bag of celery and carrots and a can of tomato juice.

"New diet." She looked longingly at the smoosh of broccoli-rice casserole on my plate. And believe me, you have to be starving to look longingly at that slop.

Denise arrived seconds before I launched into my "you don't need to be on a diet" speech. She was accompanied by Ronald, and a sense of outrage.

"You'll never guess what I heard?" Denise slammed her tray onto the table, causing her dinner roll to tumble invitingly towards Susan.

"It's bad," said Ronald, "the worst! Man, nothing like this would happen in New York."

Rhonda pointed her fork at him. "Why are you invading my lunch, Ronald? It's bad enough I have to live with you."

"It's a free country, Cuz. And besides, I'm here to testify that everything Denise heard is true."

"How do you know?"

"Because I heard it too. When I was in the office. Go ahead, Denise."

"Thanks, Ronald." She looked straight at me and shook her head. I knew it was bad because she didn't giggle once. "They're not letting us wear our uniforms on gameday."

"What? That's bullshit," Susan said.

Everyone swore up a blue streak, except Charity Louise, though she looked like she wanted to.

I sat silently, trying to make sense of Denise's words. Finally, I said, "But...that's impossible. I just talked to Wendy this morning, and she didn't say a word about it. Are they cancelling the pep rally?"

"Pep rally's still on," said Ronald.

"But how? How can they have a pep rally without uniforms?"

"Oh, there will be uniforms."

"But you said—"

"Guinevere, you're missing the point." Denise's steely eyes bored into mine. "Everyone else will be wearing their uniforms. Just not us." She pointed around the table to the members of our squad.

Understanding hit me like a missed volleyball. I turned to look at the center of the cafeteria, where Wendy held court. She was laughing with the "angle squad" girls, and I wondered if she was laughing at me.

"Was Mrs. Walters in the office when you were there?" Somehow, I already knew the answer.

"Got it in one," Ronald said as he shoveled a forkful of casserole into his mouth.

The unfairness of it boiled my blood. I sat there simmering. I knew what the old Guinevere would do when faced with injustice, but what about the new, improved Guinevere?

I stabbed at the blob of food on my plate, imagining each mushy broccoli flower was Mrs. Walters' face.

My squad grew silent as they watched me.

"Are you OK?" Denise asked.

"Why aren't you making a scene? Coming up with an impractical solution? It's eerie," said Susan.

I stood up. I suddenly knew what new Guinevere would do—and it was the same thing as the old one.

"Come on. Let's find Mr. Duncan." I left my tray on the table and started walking.

"A rumble. Sounds like fun," Ronald said, grabbing his roll for the road.

"But I haven't finished my lunch," Susan moaned.

"It's carrot sticks. They're portable," I called over my shoulder.

The whole crew followed me out of the cafeteria. Matt was coming in the door when we were going out. I invited him to join us with a brisk, "Are you in?"

"Why not? Wasn't hungry anyway." He shrugged.

The nine of us crowded into the office: me, Susan, Denise, Charity Louise, Jerica, Rhonda, Tonya, Ronald, and Matt.

The two secretaries sat gaping at their desks. Mrs. Walters, who volunteered in the office most days so she could hear all the juicy gossip, stood at the mimeograph machine. The sour smell of the ink couldn't match the sourness of her expression.

We spotted Mr. Duncan, the principal, through the open door of his office before he could close it. He snuffed his cigarette in the ashtray on his desk and came out to talk to us.

"Remind me what your name is?" he asked me.

"Guinevere MacKenzie."

"Oh, yes. You're the one who won the spelling bee last year."

"That's right."

"What can I help you with, Miss Mackenzie?"

This was my moment. I revved myself up to speak for the Pomsters and all the downtrodden students in the school. I peeked at Mrs. Walters out of the corner of my eye. She had something to do with this situation. I knew it.

"Tell him," Ronald encouraged me.

"Don't hold back," Jerica seconded.

I squared my pink-clothed shoulders and looked down at the green alligator on my breast for confidence.

"Principal Duncan, this is not a time for inaction. There is injustice here, and we will stay until you hear our voice, for we speak as one. Extra homework, cafeteria duty, none are too high a price to pay."

"Whoa, now," said Matt.

I glared at him. "I know not what course others may take, but as for me, give me fairness or give me detention. I cannot keep back my opinions even if it means sweeping the stairs in the main hall as punishment."

"Go easy, G. Nobody wants that," Susan hissed.

But I would not be silenced.

"Yes, all men—and women—are created equal. Football players and the band, equal. Cheerleaders and Pomsters, equal. We all contribute to the team, to the victory of the mighty Panthers, and we all have the right to life, liberty, and to wearing our uniforms on game day."

"Praise you, Jesus!" Charity Louise raised her hands.

"I do kinda feel like I went to church," said one of the secretaries.

I peeked at Mrs. Walters. She looked like someone had waved a tray of cafeteria broccoli under her nose.

Mr. Duncan loosened his tie. "Let me get this straight. You are all members of the pom squad, correct?"

"Yes," we said in unison.

Except Matt and Ronald. "Not us."

Mr. Duncan cricked his neck. We heard his vertebrae pop. "And you want to wear your uniforms on game day, correct?"

"Yes," we said, even Matt and Ronald.

"I don't see why not. Wear your uniforms. But now, go back to class."

A simultaneous cheer and calls of "Thank you, Mr. Duncan," were heard as we turned to leave the office.

"Miss MacKenzie."

I turned to face my principal, my king, for letting us wear our uniforms just like the cheerleaders. "Yes, Mr. Duncan?"

"Next time, you don't need a production. Just ask. That's what most people do."

And I suddenly felt very small at this reminder that I was not like most people. I slunk into the hall after my friends.

So much for the new and improved Guinevere.

Chapter 16

You May Be Right (I'm Definitely Crazy)

In the hall outside the principal's office, Ronald held up his hand, and I gave him five. I was grateful for the support, despite my misgivings about my speech, which was possibly over the top, now that I thought about it.

He was all charged up. "Man, that was theatre! Sheer theatre! You should go on the stage."

"No, she should run for StuCo, that's what she should do," said Rhonda. She had stopped in front of the bulletin board, where a large notice about the upcoming Student Council elections was posted.

"What? Me?" I stared at the flyer calling for candidates. I'd never even considered running for Student Council.

But it was flattering that Rhonda thought I should run, and I could never resist flattery. And besides, what was more normal than student government? Well, cheerleading was, but that was out as a possibility for me this year.

"Yeah," said Jerica. "One of us needs to run so this crap won't happen again. And you have the biggest mouth. You'd be perfect."

I ignored the comment about my big mouth, not only because it was unflattering, but because I was deep into imagining the possibilities of this Student Council thing.

Matt smiled like I was crazy, but he liked it.

"Go for it, girl! This lame school needs to be shook up." Ronald clapped his hands like that was that.

Susan stood back, lips locked. I couldn't read her expression. She didn't look supportive exactly, but she wasn't discouraging either.

If I'd had half a brain cell, I'd have asked what she was thinking.

Ronald said my speech was theatre, but I knew what it really was: loud and noisy. And I'd done it in front of Mrs. Walters for Heaven's sake. It was the exact opposite of what the new and improved me was aiming for. Instead of blending in with the student body, here I was standing out like a chicken in a fox den, and if I wasn't careful, I'd be eaten.

I never could back away from a mistake, though. Instead, I doubled down in a rash attempt to fix things. Maybe one day I'd learn, but it wasn't that day. I'd already decided I was running.

Denise twisted the hem of her shirt. "I don't know if you should. You know who you'll be running against, don't you?"

I did. Wendy and her minions. And I didn't care.

I pictured her hugging her mom, whispering in her ear before we came into the building that morning. It was right after I told her pom was wearing their uniforms on gameday. I'd bet a gazillion dollars that she told her mom to do something to stop us. What kind of friend does that?

As to my list, I'd already crossed Wendy off once, so I could do it again. And it wasn't being a jerk to run for office, so you could speak up for your friends.

Before I could change my mind, I marched straight back into the office. I held out my hand.

"Student Council form, please."

The secretary's eyes flashed with interest. "Which office?"

I took one look at Mrs. Walters and her disapproving smirk, then raised my chin.

"President!"

THE NEXT TWO WEEKS were the busiest of my life.

Most importantly, we had our first pep rally and football game. The student body's minds were blown when we debuted our "Funkytown" routine. After our smooth moves, the cheerleader's same-old cheers looked old-fashioned.

And the football game? I'd never forget dancing under the stadium lights on the fifty-yard line, not even if I lived to be one hundred. It was so amazing, I couldn't remember anything else about the game except for Matt running down the field in his tight white pants. Mom didn't come, of course, and neither did Dad, but it didn't matter.

I was so busy that I could almost ignore the fact that Wendy and the cheerleaders weren't speaking to me. I could almost ignore that Ronnie Mills was going around saying my name sounded like a disease. And that lots of people had started repeating him.

But what they failed to understand was that under my Student Council administration, power wouldn't be taken from the cheerleaders and football players; it would just be spread around a little so other groups could have some too.

I'd finally paid off Mamaw for my pom uniform, so I was able to invest my earnings in poster and button-making supplies. I was up to my eyeballs in magic markers, rubber cement, and glitter.

My English teacher, Mrs. Greenberg, let us use her room after school one day to work.

Matt couldn't stay because he had football practice.

Tonya was hanging out with her new boyfriend. We didn't ask what "hanging out" entailed.

And Susan had to babysit. It seemed like every time I mentioned the StuCo race, Susan was busy.

"What are we gonna put on these buttons?" Denise asked.

I struck a presidential pose. "Guinevere for the common good."

It was silent as they pondered the beauty of my slogan.

Finally, Charity Louise spoke up. "It will take a miracle to get all that on this little button, and don't you think God has more important things to do?"

"I hate to admit it, but Charity Louise is right. For once," said Jerica.

"Well then, how about 'Unity, Peace, and Guinevere'?"

"Girl, we're going to be lucky just to get your name on this thing. It's as long as I am tall."

Denise shrugged to confirm the sad truth. She picked up a pencil and began writing.

"It's not as long as Charity Louise," said Charity Louise, trying to make me feel better. It didn't work.

"How about this?" Denise held up a paper that said, Vote 4 Guinevere.

"It's not very inspiring."

Denise looked disappointed by my lack of enthusiasm.

"But it's straightforward. Easy to understand," said Ronald.

Denise gave him a thankful smile.

Charity Louise popped the cap off a purple marker and got to work. "And most importantly, it will fit on the buttons.

Like Kenny Rogers said, you have to know when to fold them. So, I did. "It's great. I love it. Thanks Denise. Let's get to work. We only have the room for about 40 more minutes."

The markers squeaked. Their pungent odor filled the air, making us all a little high. We joked about it, and the laughter helped push away some of the anxiety we all felt that I was going to lose to Wendy, and lose big.

A knock on the door frame sobered us up fast. But it wasn't a teacher, it was a group of two boys and three girls.

"Hey, we heard you were working on campaign stuff. Do you need help?" asked one of the boys.

"Well, yes. But, just to be clear," I said, "this is the GUINEVERE for President campaign. Do you still want to help?"

"Yeah. Anything to keep Wendy Walters from winning again," said a girl.

My friends and I shared excited glances. Maybe I wouldn't lose too big. Maybe I could win this thing. We gave the newcomers markers and buttons and let them get to work.

"Have you decided what you're going to say in your speech?" Rhonda asked.

"Yeah, what do you stand for? Other than the little man?" Ronald stood up and put his thumbs behind his rainbow-striped Mork from Ork suspenders. He was undoubtedly short.

"I have ideas, big ideas, but they're still formulating. I'll keep them secret until the speech."

Denise got a sudden case of hiccups; the first she'd had in a while. "No. *Hic.* Guinevere. That's a bad idea. *Hic.*"

Jerica wagged her finger at me. "Don't go promising crap you can't do. No matter how much we want it, they're not going to allow carnival rides on the sports field for homecoming. That's just in the movies."

"And don't try to be a dictator," Charity Louise said. "This is America."

"Good point. What do you all want me to do?"

"We want you to beat Wendy," said one of the new kids, "Whatever it takes."

"She's run things for long enough," said another.

"Or her mom has, but it's the same thing really," said a third.

I spent the next twenty minutes listening to my future constituents.

MOMENTUM BUILT. AN ARMY of kids, some I'd never met, handed out Vote 4 Guinevere buttons. My Pomsters plastered the halls with my posters.

All except Susan. She said she was busy. It was almost like she didn't want me to be president.

Wendy walked around at a constant simmer, just waiting to boil over.

The cheerleaders were strung so tight that a Herkie would launch them into the stratosphere.

Ronnie Mills and the football players—all except Matt, who was helping me, but in secret—had switched from saying my name sounded like a disease to saying I *was* a disease. Not going to lie, I didn't like it, but I figured I'd take care of it later, after I won the presidency.

I used a permanent marker to scratch Wendy off my list. It wasn't that I didn't like her, because believe it or not, I did. But it was like Susan said, if you weren't useful to her, she turned on you. Judging by the student body's response to my campaign, though, I was on my way to becoming normal without her.

On Thursday, two weeks after the first day of school, the day I'd won a victory for the pom squad's right to wear their uniforms—and embarrassed myself in the process—election day arrived.

I consulted the latest issue of *Seventeen* and dressed in my presidential best: grey blazer, navy blue knee-length skirt, and a lavender high-collared blouse with a purple grosgrain-ribbon tie. But looking the part didn't mean I felt it.

I felt like I was going to barf, especially when I saw Wendy all decked out in her cheerleading outfit. She'd applied glittery roll-on gel to her eyelids and perfectly shaved legs so she would shimmer under the spotlight. It had never occurred to me to wear my pom uniform – or glitter. I looked like the ancient librarian. *Seventeen* had let me down.

From backstage, I peeked through the curtains and watched as the auditorium seats filled. Rhonda, Jerica, Charity Louise, and Ronald snagged seats in the front row. Matt was about halfway back in the center section. The lights glinted off his blonde curls. I didn't see Susan or Denise anywhere.

Excited murmuring filled the air, like people were going to a party instead of a school assembly. Maybe they were interested in seeing me get creamed, like a bunch of Romans going to the Colosseum to see Christians get eaten by lions. Or maybe they were amped up because they wanted me to win.

A girl could hope.

The candidates for Parliamentarian went first, followed by Sergeant at Arms and all the rest. I was too nervous to listen, which was weird. I was never nervous when I did the spelling bee or when I played small parts in the school plays. But then, I wasn't going up against Wendy. Spelling bees and plays were beneath her.

The presidential speeches were last. First her. Then me.

Her speech was short and sweet. Basically, she talked about how great she was and how great the Homecoming Dance would be if she were in charge of it. It got a smattering of applause, especially from the center section where the football players sat.

But when I walked from the wings to the podium at center stage, the crowd cheered. I froze and looked over my shoulder, wondering if Michael Jackson or someone had walked in behind me.

They were clapping for me. I couldn't believe it.

I made my way to the podium and looked out at the sea of faces. Hundreds of faces. I froze again, grasping at the words that had flown right out of my head. I had to say something, though, so I said the first thing that popped into my brain.

"Wocka-wocka-wocka!"

The raucous noise cooled almost to silence.

"Well, I guess there are no Fozzie Bear fans here."

Someone shouted from the very back of the auditorium. "Why did the chicken cross the playground?"

"Ha! There's one, at least. To get to the other slide." I tapped a rim shot on the podium. *Ba-dum-tshh.*

The crowd squirmed in their seats. Seemed like I'd gotten off on the wrong foot. I needed to recalibrate.

"Hey guys, Guinevere MacKenzie here—not to tell you jokes, rare or otherwise, but to convince you to vote for me to be your next Student Council President.

"Beat Wendy!" an anonymous person called. Enthusiastic clapping spread across the room.

I glimpsed Wendy glaring at me from the wings like she was trying to hex me. I would not let her.

"Alright. I can tell you're ready for a change. You're ready for 'Unity, Peace, and Guinevere.'"

On the front row, my friends rolled their eyes, all except Ronald, who tried to lead the crowd in chanting "Unity, Peace, and Guinevere," until Rhonda elbowed him in the stomach.

"Too early in the morning for chants, I guess," I mumbled as I fished my crumpled speech from the pocket of my blazer. Improvisation was doing me no favors. The microphone picked up the crackle of the notebook paper as I tried to smooth it out. I squinted through the harsh glare of the spotlight at the barest of bare outlines for my speech:

- Slogan

- Ronald Reagan

- Serve my constituents

- THE PLAN

Too late, I realized I'd been overconfident. When I'd practiced my speech in front of the mirror at home, it was easy. But standing there in front of my classmates,

I couldn't remember who Ronald Reagan was, let alone why he was on my list.

Wendy's lips turned up in the hint of a smile.

"Anyway, I am deeply aware that being Student Council President is a big responsibility and if elected, I will live up to the demands expected of me and earn your trust—"

"Beat Wendy," someone yelled.

"I'm trying." I laughed, but it was annoying; they'd thrown me off my stride. I took a breath. "More than anything, I want to be president to unify our school, to bring all the different groups together, so that 'Mighty Panthers' can be more than a cheer. It will be a reality." The words I'd practiced started coming back to me.

"They tell us that it's normal for some groups to be higher than other groups because that's the way it's always been—"

"I'm high, but I don't care."

"Who gives a toke?"

"Let's roll, baby!"

The crowd laughed at the hecklers. I was losing my audience. Time to get to the point.

"They say, 'It was good enough for us, it should be good enough for you.'

"They expect that we'll stay in our groups, in our individual lanes, and accept the way things have always been.

"But my fellow Panthers, I reject that view. Every group at West Junior High is—and should be—equal."

The crowd cheered. I'd won them back. It was time to unveil my grand plan.

"Which is why I'm announcing the biggest part of my presidential platform. After talking to my future constituents, I know everyone wants a change—"

"Yes, we do!"

"Bring it on!"

I had them. Wendy was biting her pink-polished fingernail.

"And so, to create this change and build unity among all the students, once a week, the cafeteria table groups will be broken up and assigned random seating. Band members will sit with football players. Pom squad with cheerleaders. Introverts with extroverts. And nobody will sit alone. We will get to know each other. And when we do, peace will reign in the hallways and classrooms of our school."

"Aw, man!"

"No!"

"Not that!"

"Crap-ola!"

I had to admit, my announcement didn't get the reaction I'd hoped.

Stunned silence reigned in the auditorium.

Rhonda's head was in her lap.

Ronald's hand was over his mouth.

Jerica stared at the ceiling.

Charity Louise gave a nervous round of applause that hung in the silence like microphone feedback, making everyone cringe.

Susan and Denise were still nowhere in sight.

And a look of devilish joy crossed Wendy's face.

I'd sorely miscalculated. Apparently, lunch seating wasn't the kind of change people wanted. If I were normal, I might have figured that out before humiliating myself.

But I couldn't just walk off the stage without finishing. I cut to the end.

"So, in the spirit of unity and peace, I ask for your vote. Thank you."

A couple of years before, Dad went out to L.A. to try to make it as a comedian. He told me this story about how bad he bombed his first set and ended up selling his jokes in the parking lot to another comedian for a pack of cigarettes and $25.

This was like that. I walked off the stage to spurts of laughter popcorning across the auditorium.

From the wings, I watched Mr. Brown, the StuCo sponsor, give instructions about voting. Suddenly, Denise was there, clutching my arm.

She whispered, "Come with me. I'm sorry. So sorry."

"What?"

"I've got a pass." She waved it in front of my face. "Office."

I stared at the white slip of paper: Guinevere MacKenzie to Main Office. It was signed by Principal Duncan.

Great. My second trip to the principal's office in two weeks. Freshman year was getting off to a fantastic start. And if you didn't guess, that's sarcasm.

DENISE HICCUPPED DOWN THE hall. I followed, two steps behind, my thoughts turned inward. Maybe I still had a chance of winning the election, but it felt like I'd blown it. People didn't know a great idea even when it hit them in the face. And why was I being called to the principal's office? Did Mr. Duncan have something against Fozzie Bear?

"Susan discovered them." Denise's statement caught my attention.

"What did she discover?"

"Your posters."

"What's wrong with my posters? Did someone use the wrong kind of tape to hang them on the walls or something?"

"Worse. They got vandalized. Whoever did it was mean. Of course, we don't know who it was, but—"

"We can guess."

"Yep. Susan pulled them off the wall before too many people saw them. I helped a little, but by the time I got there, she was pretty much done."

Susan's voice carried into the hall as we approached the principal's office.

"Oh, come on, it's obvious who did it."

"We have no evidence, Miss Jackson. I'll ask around, try to find out if there are witnesses, but I can't accuse students without evidence," Mr. Duncan said in a tired voice that sounded like he was sick to death of being principal.

When I walked through the door, he was rubbing the top of his head. Maybe he hoped that, like Aladdin's lamp, a genie would appear to get him out of there.

My posters were wadded up and stuffed in one of the tall, narrow trash cans that were standard issue in all the classrooms. I caught the letters G-E-R written in black, wide-tipped marker on one. I bit the inside of my lip, pulled it from the cam, and flattened it out.

"Germevere! Don't catch the disease!"

The scrawl obscured my carefully lettered slogan.

I pulled out the next poster. And the next.

"Don't G," Susan said, "they're all the same."

But a perverse impulse made me look. She was right, the idiots had no originality. But what they'd written was bad enough. "Germevere!" It was like being shunned when I had lice that time, all over again.

"Thanks for taking them down," I said to Susan.

"Of course."

My heart swelled with love at her declaration that taking them down was the only option. That's what friends did. I'd do it for them, too. No questions asked.

"I'm sorry this happened, Miss Mackenzie," Principal Duncan said as he picked up the posters and crammed them back in the trash can. Judging by the way he squinted his eyes, the sight of them gave him a headache.

"What happens now?" I asked. "Are you going to stop the voting?"

He pursed his lips. "No. I don't think anyone saw the posters. Delaying the election won't make a difference in the result."

"But—"

"I'll try to find out what happened. And if I do, the culprits will be punished. Unfortunately, these things happen."

"They shouldn't."

"I agree. Miss Jackson here suggested we let you know before the students were dismissed from the assembly, and I thought it was an excellent idea. But now, I hear the approaching stampede. It's time to go to class."

The posters were wadded up in the can, but I could still picture the writing. Germevere. I knew I wasn't all that great. I mean, my parents didn't even want to be around me more than they had to, but to be labelled a disease was even lower than my own low opinion of myself. I'd always known that Wendy and her minions thought I was weird, but being weird was a million times better than being contagious.

"I can't."

"You can't what, Miss MacKenzie?"

"I can't go to class. I think I have a fever. I need to go home."

Denise patted me on the back.

Mr. Duncan swiveled his neck to release the tension. "Go over to the nurse. She'll call your mom."

Long story short, the nurse called Mom, who signed me out on the phone, and I walked home because I wasn't sick; it was only my heart that was sore.

At my house, I cleaned my room because that always made me feel better. Then I crashed on my bed and stared up at the Scott Baios. To be honest, even though that's where my eyes were focused, I didn't see them. I just kept thinking about my speech and those posters.

How had I gotten things so wrong?

Why did I always get everything wrong?

The answer was seared onto my retinas. Despite all my efforts to remake myself into the normal girl God intended me to be, I was a germ. Doomed from the start. Thwarted by my weirdo parents, my grody appearance, and my strange name. If things were ever going to change—if I was going to change—I'd have to try a lot harder.

A knock on the front door jerked me out of my pity party, but not out of my funk. It was Susan. I almost never let my friends come over because Mom's parts of the house were always a mess, but I let her in and shuffled her into my bedroom before she could get a glimpse of the cat-hair-covered cat palace.

"Whoa! It's lemony in here," Susan said as I closed my door.

"Lemon Pledge. Scent of the gods." I pulled out the stool from under the vanity table that Gerald made for me. "Have a seat." I collapsed onto my bed.

"So, still obsessed with Chachi, I see."

"Don't beat around the bush, Susan. I lost, right?"

"You lost."

"How bad was it?"

"Well, West Junior High is not exactly NBC, so they don't tell you the percentages and stuff, but when I was at my locker, I overheard someone say that they'd overheard one of the office secretaries say that it was bad."

"I knew it. I can't believe I thought I had a chance."

"You did have a chance, until you came out with that craptacular idea. Seriously, nobody wants that. People just like to sit with their friends."

I wanted it. I couldn't be the only one. There was something else involved, and I thought I knew. "I know why they didn't vote for me."

"You mean something besides your lame-ass idea?"

"It's my name. I've been thinking about this for a while, but I've finally decided. I'm changing it."

Susan banged the back of her head on my wall. Repeatedly.

"You don't think it's a good idea."

"I don't understand why you keep putting your neck out. For someone who says they just want to fit in, you sure make yourself stick out in a crowd."

"Believe me, I'm trying to be normal."

"You don't have to be normal. Who the hell cares if you're normal? Be as weird as you want, but stop giving people a target."

I pushed the spiral notebook with my list under the pillow. I hadn't talked to Susan about my goals because I knew she'd react exactly like she was reacting.

It suddenly dawned on me why I hadn't seen much of her the last two weeks. "That's why you didn't help with the campaign, isn't it? Because when I stick my head out, it exposes you too."

She shrugged, rolling her eyes to the ceiling. "I've been busy. I told you when I got crowned that I'd be doing more stuff with my tribe."

"Oh yeah. You did. That's so great. I wish you'd reminded me. I thought you weren't around because you didn't want me to run."

She turned to straighten the snapshots I'd wedged around the vanity mirror. "I feel like I'm being smothered by a king-sized lemon pillow in here. Why don't we walk over to the football field to watch practice? That will cheer you up."

"Ooh! Matt in white pants. That would cheer anyone up."

As I opened my bedroom door, being careful not to let the cats in, Susan put her hand on my shoulder. "G, do me a favor. Please! Keep your head down. At least for a while."

"OK, I will. If you do me a favor, too. Call me Martha."

Susan groaned and walked out the door.

Chapter 17

A Rose by Any Other Name

Susan was right when she told me to stop being Wendy's flunky and ordered me not to do her homework anymore. And she was right about keeping my head down after the election disaster.

Or at least, I was pretty sure she was.

I told the Pomsters about my name change right away. They rolled their eyes but accepted my wishes. Sure, they slipped up sometimes, but if I wanted to be Martha, they weren't going to argue. Too much, anyway.

Coach Jamey said, "I understand wanting to make a new start," which was one of many reasons I loved her.

My mom refused to call me anything other than the name she had chosen. Not even after I tried to guilt trip her about the fact she hadn't come to a game to watch the pom squad yet.

I didn't bother telling those wonderful old stick-in-the-muds, Mamaw and Gerald, about my name change, not even when I spent all day Saturday going through Mamaw's fabric stack, looking for a piece I could use to sew a dress for the homecoming dance. Not even when they drove me to the fabric store to buy a dress pattern and then stopped off to get burgers at the burger stand. I didn't tell them, and I wouldn't. What was the point?

And I hadn't talked to Dad in like three weeks. So, likewise, what was the point?

I did such a good job of keeping my head down that my classmates didn't know I'd changed my name for three whole school days. When I went back to school after the election, most people avoided me because I'd dashed their hopes for change and doomed them to another year of a Wendy Walters administration.

Since I always did what I was supposed to in class, the teachers didn't have reason to call on me. And there was no need to talk to Wendy. She just smirked a superior smile that she'd bested me once again.

At least she called off her toadies. Nobody called me Germevere anymore. Not to my face, anyway. But the sting lingered.

Finally, on the third day after the election, in English class, Mrs. Greenberg called on me to explain why Dimmesdale is such a jerk to Hester in *The Scarlet Letter*. When I said, "Call me Martha, please," my classmates laughed like changing my name was exactly what they'd expect from someone who wanted to upset the settled cafeteria seating order. Then they went about their day, not thinking about it at all.

I was disappointed my name change didn't make more of a stir. It made me doubt Susan's usual good advice. It made me question my long-standing belief that my transformation from hopeless freakazoid to total normality required losing myself in the crowd.

Being invisible sucked, at home and school and everywhere.

And besides, Wendy was the most normal person I knew, and she was front and center in pretty much everything. I wanted to be like Wendy but nicer.

For the next few days, as I reminded everyone to call me Martha, Susan's request that I stay under the radar, and my fear that doing it would make me even more invisible than

I already was, battled it out in my fitful brain, my battered soul, and my nauseated stomach.

And then, like a sign from God, an opportunity crossed my path to put my restless thoughts to the test. To decide the matter once and for all.

One of the best things about being an aide for Mrs. Greenberg, who was not only the English teacher but also the sponsor of a bunch of school activities, including the annual talent show, was finding out what was happening before most of the other students. When she asked me to mimeograph 20 copies of the Homecoming Talent Show announcement and hang them around the school before I walked to my Geometry class, it gave me a jump on the competition. First prize was a gift certificate to Anthony's Department Store and a pass to the local bowling alley, but more than that, winning would give me a chance to redeem myself in the eyes of the student body after my failed presidential bid.

As I pinned and taped the notices up, I thought about what act I could do for the talent show.

By the time I hung the last mimeograph copy on the bulletin board next to the cafeteria line and dashed out the door to walk to the high school for my class, I knew what I was going to do.

It was a brilliant idea, if I could find a Romeo. I knew who I wanted it to be, but would he do it? Well, a faint heart never won fair Romeo, so I had to ask.

I cornered Matt in the barfeteria, which was easy because he was sitting at the corner of his usual table.

"Ehh. What's up, Doc?"

He laughed and scooted over so I could squeeze one butt cheek onto the bench. It was enough.

"Not much, you wascally wabbit. What's up with you?"

"News! There's going to be a talent show."

"So?"

"So, I have a great idea for an act and I'm making you an offer you can't refuse—a chance to be in it."

He snort-laughed. "What are you suggesting? A clarinet duet? Unfortunately—Not!—I sold mine back to the music store."

"No, this is bigger than clarinets. Picture it. You, me, Shakespeare, the balcony scene from Romeo and Juliet. You'd be Romeo. Though if you want to do a kind of cross-dressing thing and be Juliet, I could go for that. But I already know Juliet's lines. What do you think?"

I had rendered Matt speechless. He stared at me like I was crazy for a solid minute, and if you've ever had someone stare at you for a whole minute, you'll know that's longer than it sounds.

"Guin…Martha, that's insane. I wouldn't do it for a million dollars."

"Ah, come on. It'll be fun." I punched him in the arm to rally him to my cause.

"I'd rather go to a prayer meeting with Charity Louise."

"Ooh! That bad, huh?"

"Yep. Good luck, though."

No sense pressing my luck. "Thanks. I'd better get my food before the cafeteria ladies close the line."

It was too bad. Matt would have been a cute Romeo, especially if he wore tights and a short tunic so you could see his butt. But I wasn't giving up on the scheme because I knew I'd be a great Juliet.

Denise wouldn't do it, which was good because she'd be so adorable that nobody would notice I was on stage. Maybe I could talk Susan into it.

I plopped my Salisbury Mystery Meat with mashed potatoes on the table across from her. "Still eating rabbit food?"

She viciously chomped a celery stick.

"Tetchy-tetchy. I've got something to cheer you up. Did you see the notice about the talent show?"

She smiled, a good sign. "Yeah, I did. I was—"

"I have the BEST idea for an act. We could do the balcony scene from Romeo and Juliet. One of us would need to be Romeo. You or me, I don't care. Though I already know Juliet's lines."

"Actually, I was—"

"It will be great. I'm not sure what we'll do about a balcony, but we'll figure it out. Maybe a—"

"No!"

"What?"

"I said, no. I already have an idea for the talent show."

"Oh." I mixed the gravy into the potatoes.

"Don't you want to know what it is?"

"Of course, I do."

"I'm going to dance. I'm supposed to do things to promote my Native culture. This is a good opportunity."

"You're going to dance by yourself?"

"Yes. You'll have to find someone else to be Romeo." She tore my roll in half and took a bite.

Before I could ask them, the Pomsters spoke up.

"Don't look at me."

"Me either."

"No way."

"Acting's a sin."

To give me time to think, I stuffed the other half of the roll into my mouth. It was a big step for Susan. I should be happy for her. What was I saying? I WAS happy for her. I choked down the roll. "It's an amazing idea, Susan! You're going to be great.

While everyone asked Susan what she would wear for her performance, I considered my next move. I was proud that she'd found the courage to get up there on her own, but I wasn't giving up my plans. There was room for both of us.

"Uh-hum." Ronald slid onto the bench beside me. "Hear you're looking for a Romeo."

"Yeah."

"Well, look no further. I'm your man."

"You want to be my Romeo?" I swear, Ronald was always flirting with me. I was worried he liked me. And while he was nice and all, and he certainly had flair, he was also a foot shorter than I was. But I didn't want to hurt his feelings. "What are your leading man qualifications?"

"You heard of that *Fame* movie?"

"Of course, I have! Man, I'd love to go to a school like that." I started singing, "Fame! I'm gonna live forever—"

"Enough. I don't think you've got a triple threat going on."

"Ha, you're right. More like a threat-threat."

"Well, I got into that school before my family decided to send me here. But if you watched the movie, you know it's hard to get in. That's my qualification."

Wow! My only acting experience was bit parts in three school plays, though I did have lines in two of them. Ronald's resume was legit!

"You and me, Guinevere—"

"Martha."

"You and me, Martha, we'll win first prize."

With visions of earning the respect of the student body in my eyes, I stretched out my hand. "It's a deal, Ronald. You, me, and Shakespeare for the win."

WITH ONLY TWO WEEKS before the show, we had to get right to work. Finding a place to rehearse was a challenge. Obviously, we couldn't use my house; there was too much to explain. And we couldn't use his house because he said his family were lunatics. We settled on practicing outside at the rec center.

Luckily, it stayed warm way into October in Tulsa, so warm that I had to convince Ronald to take off the puffer jacket he always wore. He was not going to die of heat stroke on my watch. He said in New York City, it was already getting cold this time of year. He said he wore the jacket to remember his life there.

The park had picnic tables that I could stand on to pretend I was on a balcony. Luckily, I already knew all of Juliet's lines. The challenge was letting Ronald say Romeo's because in my bedroom, I usually played both parts.

We practiced about a million times, but we didn't practice the kiss. I felt weird about it. Number one, because it was Ronald, and I was pretty sure he was madly in love with me. I didn't want to encourage him. But also, because the only person I'd ever kissed was Timmy, but we were only five years old, so it didn't count. I had no experience, and Ronald probably had a ton, being from New York and all. I didn't want to make a fool of myself.

"Damn it, Guinevere—"

"Martha."

"Damn it, Martha. We got to practice the kiss. I don't want our first time to be in front of the whole school."

"I know, I know." I jumped up and down on top of the picnic table. It rocked a little too much, so I sat down and dangled my legs over the side. Ronald hopped up on the table beside me.

"Why are you afraid. Is it because I'm Black? Better not be. If it is, you sure have fooled me because I thought you were better than that."

"No, Ronald. I don't care that you're Black." Though I was guessing my Mamaw would. "It's just that I've noticed since you moved here that you pay a lot of attention to me, and I don't want you to get the wrong idea."

Ronald lay back on the table and put his hands behind his head. "Damn. You think I like you?" He laughed.

Not going to lie, the laugh didn't do much for my ego. "Don't you?"

"Well, I like you and all, but—"

"You don't like me-like me."

"No. Sorry to bust your bubble."

"Oh."

He sat back up. "I'm sorry. I thought you knew." He lowered his voice to a whisper, "I don't like girls."

I stared blankly at him for a minute, and then it hit me. "Oh. Oooooh!! I see. You mean, you're like—"

"Now you got it."

"Like the Village People."

He laughed again. "You're one weird chick. You've probably never met anyone like me, around here."

"You'd be surprised."

"No way! Who?"

"Promise you won't tell?"

"If you promise not to tell on me."

"Of course I won't. Friends don't snitch." It was my turn to whisper. "It's my dad."

"No kidding?"

"No kidding. It's kind of a new thing for him. I'm still getting used to it. But I never guessed about you."

"It's why my family sent me here. Caught me kissing a boy. They figured living in Oklahoma would whip some sense into me, which proves my family knows nothing about nothing."

"I understand. Same with mine."

Ronald started laughing. "Damn, you thought I had a thing for you! I know who you've got a thing for."

"Bet you don't."

"You think I'm blind. You've got the hots for Matt, don't you."

"Is it that obvious?"

"Plain as day. You going to the dance with him?"

"I doubt it. I'm making a dress to dazzle him though. If I finish it." Boy, I'd thought I was being subtle, but apparently not. I'd be so embarrassed if news of my crush got round to Matt. "Ronald, please don't tell anyone."

"I won't tell. You might want to control your hungry eyes, though. Can we practice the kiss?"

"Sure."

There weren't fireworks or anything, but it was alright. Though I did suggest that next time he use some lip balm. At least we wouldn't be nervous during the talent show.

THURSDAY NIGHT WAS THE homecoming game. The Pomsters passed our pompoms to the beat of Billy Joel. The audience cheered because we were amazing. My mom didn't come, and neither did Dad. Wendy was crowned junior varsity homecoming queen.

The talent show was held in the auditorium on Friday. I invited Mom, but I knew she wouldn't take off work for it.

Wendy wore her crown and sat in the place of honor with King Ronnie and the rest of the homecoming court in the center of the front row. Her mom sat off to the side, clicking her camera like a paparazzi.

Many different singers sang to honor the royal court. A few of them could sing. A seventh-grade girl played the accordion, which was, shall we say, interesting. Another kid juggled. A group of girls jumped rope and were so amazing, I figured they'd win. But I hadn't counted on Susan.

Susan's uncle beat the drum while she danced across the stage, suddenly graceful like I'd never known her to be. I got lost in the rhythm of the drum and the fluttering fringe of her shawl. My foul-mouthed, tell-it-like-it-is friend moved as delicately as a butterfly. It was the most beautiful thing I'd ever seen, and I knew right away that Ronald and I were going to lose. I was completely OK with that, though, because Susan was going to win and I loved her.

When she finished, the audience gave her a standing ovation. From backstage, I clapped like one of those wind-up monkeys; on and on and on.

Once the stage was clear and the audience had settled down, two guys from the stage crew set up my tower at center stage. It was only a tall folding ladder that I talked the custodian into loaning us, but I knew it would work because Mom had taken me to a free play at the junior college where there was nothing on stage except ladders and chairs, and it was spectacular.

I climbed up the ladder in one of Mamaw's long, lacy nightgowns. I halfway wondered why Mamaw had such a fancy nightgown, but sometimes it's best not to think about stuff like that. I struck my opening pose.

Delmer Dinkins and an eighth grader I didn't know were sharing the job of Master of Ceremonies. I never would have guessed Delmer had it in him to be a M.C. I suspected there was some poetic lesson in that, but I was just trying to remember my lines.

"And the last act to perform for our homecoming court is Ronald Allen and Guinevere Mackenzie, performing—"

I waved my hands and shouted down at him, "Wait, Delmer. That's not right."

He looked at me, then at his notecards, then back at me. He raised his hands, palms up, and shrugged.

I mouthed my new name. *Martha. It's Martha.*

"What?" Delmer conferred with the eigth grader. They looked offstage at Mrs. Greenberg for guidance.

Meanwhile, I climbed down from the ladder, which was a trick in my long nightie. I walked to the microphone.

"Excuse me. Thank you." I looked over the heads of the audience at the back wall and said, "It's Martha. Martha MacKenzie."

I climbed back up the ladder to the sound of muffled laughter. Delmer and the eighth grader exited the stage.

After taking a slow breath in and out to calm my beating heart, I arranged my folded arms on the ladder's top cap, tilted my head, and gazed wistfully over the heads of the audience. I pretended the spotlight that was beginning to make me sweat was a delicate twinkling star in an Italian sky.

Ronald tromped in from stage left. Somewhere, he had found a pair of knee-high boots to tuck his too-tight sweatpants into. They had a bit of a heel. I guessed he had "borrowed" them from Rhonda. I also guessed that Rhonda was going to kill him right after our scene was over.

He marched past my ladder to downstage right, peered out at the audience, then, after turning to catch a glimpse of me, gasped and placed his hands over his heart.

I kept my dreamy eyes on the moonlit sky over Verona.

ROMEO: He jests at scars that never felt a wound. But, soft! What light through yonder window breaks? It is the east, and Juliet is the sun...

It was a long speech. When we practiced at the park, I hadn't fully realized how long Romeo's speech was, but it involved a lot of sighing and staring at the stars, which Ronald was milking for all he was worth.

Meanwhile, sweat had begun beading on my forehead as I waited for the cue to raise my hand to my face.

Ronald dropped to one knee with a thud. His hand was still on his heart.

ROMEO: ...See, how she leans her cheek upon her hand! O, that I were a glove upon that hand, That I might touch that cheek!

JULIET: Ay me!

Finally, I got to say something, but it was only two words.

ROMEO: O, speak again bright angel...

I wanted to shout, *if you'd stop hamming it up, I'd be able to,* but I forced myself to stay in character until the line I'd been waiting for—the reason I'd picked this scene in the first place—was cued.

JULIET: O Romeo, Romeo! wherefore art thou, Romeo? Deny thy father and refuse thy name; Or, if thou wilt not, be but sworn my love, And I'll no longer be a Capulet.

Now we were cooking. I was surprised by how quiet the audience was. We were wowing them. I could feel the tension in the room—the good kind—as they waited to see what happened next. Despite my public upbeat statements to friends and foes, I'd had my doubts about West

Junior High's readiness for Shakespeare. I was glad to be wrong.

Ronald flapped in front of the ladder like a bird before pausing to put both his hands on his heart. Again.

> ROMEO: With love's light wings did I o'er-perch these walls; For stony limits cannot hold love out, And what love can do that dares love attempt; Therefore thy kinsman are no let to me.

I stretched out my arms, imploring him not to be rash.

> JULIET: If they do see thee, they will murder thee.

And it crossed my mind that though my classmates were holding their breath as they watched us perform Shakespeare, they might not be ready for what was coming next. It was 1981, not 1931, but our little slice of town was stuck in the past. It was too late to stop the ride though, because Ronald was climbing up the ladder towards me.

He hung off to the side, so he didn't block me from view. As he got closer, I was glad to see he'd smeared on some lip balm. It shimmered suspiciously like Tonya's Watermelon Kissing Slicks. Smelled like it too.

It was so silent in the auditorium that I could hear the droplet of sweat that dripped off my chin to splash on the ladder. I leaned towards Ronald and, in a hushed voice, said my final line.

> JULIET: Good night, good night! parting is such sweet sorrow, That I shall say good night till it be morrow.

And then he kissed me.

And then?

The audience erupted.

He never did get to say his last line.

Before I knew it, the curtain had closed.

And Susan was marching my way, fists clenched at her sides.

Chapter 18
Take Me Home, Rocky Road

"Susan, you were amazing! Absolutely beautiful!" I said, throwing my arms up to hug my friend. I meant it and was not just trying to ward off her clenched fists.

She evaded my hug and leaned towards me, hissing her frustration into my ear instead of broadcasting it to everyone, because she's decent like that, "Why do you always have to make a spectacle of yourself? You promised to keep your head down."

"I didn't make a spectacle; I just did a play. That's all. But I don't expect to win the talent show or anything because you were amazing. Really! You're going to win. You deserve to win."

"Even if I win, nobody will remember it. All they'll remember is you kissing Ronald." Her cheeks were red, and her eyes were all glassy with tears. I'd never seen her so mad, except for that day at the pool.

On the other side of the curtain, the Student Council sponsor began announcing the winners of the talent show. And then the curtain was shoved aside, and Mrs. Walters barged through, followed by her PTA lackeys.

Ronald squeezed himself between me and Susan. "Sweet, Jesus. They're going to lynch me."

"They'll have to go through me, first," I said, shielding him with my body.

"Me too. We've got your back," said Susan, standing beside me.

But Mrs. Walters didn't even look at Ronald; all her attention was focused on me. She gathered her PTA buddies around her and pointed at me, "If I've told you once, I've told you a thousand times, that girl is NOT NICE. Reading dirty books to my daughter, and kissing...well, you saw."

"Wait a minute," Susan shouted. "You have a lot of gall accusing Guinevere—"

"Martha," I whispered. But why did I bother?

"—when your daughter—"

"Excuse me!" said a cold and steely voice.

Susan and Mrs. Walters were still yelling when I realized I knew that voice.

"I said, excuse me!"

"You came!" I said to my mom.

"Yes. Your guilt trip worked." She smirked.

Despite the weird circumstances, I grinned, even though Mom was wearing an elven cloak over the scrubs she wore to work at the hospital.

She smiled back at me and then turned a frown at Mrs. Walters. Her voice was calm but dripping with poison when she said, "Why, may I ask, are you shouting at these children?"

"I second the question," said Mr. Duncan as he sidled up beside us. "Mrs. Walters, I value your volunteerism, but chastising students who have done nothing wrong won't fly here."

She snapped her mouth shut, but she was still fuming.

"Let's continue this discussion in my office, please. Miss MacKenzie, Mr. Allen. And you must be Mrs. MacKenzie." He nodded to my mom.

"Ms. But yes, I'm Guinevere's mother."

"By the way, they're calling your name to go get your award, Miss Jackson. You won. Congratulations," he said before walking away, expecting us all to follow him.

"I knew you'd win!" I flung my arms around Susan and hugged her tight.

She growled but hugged back. "You are so freaking in-furiating! It's a good thing I like you, or I'd kill you."

I laughed and followed Principal Duncan to the office for my third visit of the year.

Susan laughed and went to get her winning gift certifi-cates.

"Come on, kiddo," Mom said to Ronald. "Let's clear this mess up."

The short walk to the office was interrupted by peo-ple stopping to high-five me and Ronald, and by people giving us dirty looks. Luckily, the ratio of "awesome" to "disgusting" was tilted heavily to awesome. Ronald's smile got bigger and bigger as we walked down the hall. I was glad to discover that most of my classmates weren't like Mrs. Walters.

"Hey, Martha," Matt called, running up beside me. He had that grin on his face, like I was the weirdest person he'd ever met, but he kind of liked it. "That was so cool!"

"Sad that you passed up the opportunity, are you?"

He laughed. "Not on your life. Are you going to the dance tonight?"

I paused for a second. Was he asking me what I thought he was? "Yeah, I'm going."

"Cool. See you there."

Mom and Ronald raised their eyebrows.

In the office, Mr. Duncan said to me, "Well, Miss MacKenzie, making a stir again, I see."

Mom's eyebrow went up even higher at that. She didn't yet know how well I'd been getting to know the principal.

Mr. Duncan assured us that we weren't being punished because we'd done nothing wrong, except overacting. He also promised that he would talk to Mrs. Walters and set her straight about everything, which he inferred included her prejudice, but he didn't come right out and say that.

Mom checked me out of school for the rest of the day, which really surprised me. She said her day was shot, anyway, so why not go all in?

Made sense to me.

MOM GOT A DOUBLE dip of Rocky Road. And more than that, she got it on a delicate, pointed sugar cone.

Rocky Road always freaked me out. All those ingredients made it heavy. Too heavy. Her cone was going to break. I knew it.

I got a single dip of vanilla on a regular flat-bottomed cone; simple, uncomplicated, and sturdy.

We found a table outside and I sat, licking around the circumference of the cone to catch the drips before they dropped.

I must have looked miserable because Mom said, "You OK?"

"Not really. I think I'm cursed. I'll never be normal. Weirdness is in my genes."

"So, it's your dad's and my fault, I presume."

"Who else? You guys are like weirdness royalty."

Mom halfway smiled, like she was trying to stifle it. "Did you ever consider that most people think they're the normal ones and the rest of the world is off their rocker?"

"Except me. I know I'm weird."

"Proving my point. You are weird. Way out in right field."

"I know. I'm trying to change."

"I mean, you starch your shirts." She started giggling, and all the stress poured out of her.

I realized it was the first time in forever that I'd heard her laugh. She wiped her eyes at the thought of me starching my shirts. And even though that was the least weird thing about me, her laugh was infectious. I started giggling, too.

"What can I say? I like the crisp snap of pinpoint cotton."

"You button your top button," she guffawed.

"Well, of course. My ribbon tie hangs better that way." I patted the loops of the bow.

"Ribbon tie?!" She laughed so hard, tears leaked from the corners of her eyes.

I was getting annoyed. The tie-derision was a bit rich, coming from someone wearing an elf cloak.

"Mom! What I'm saying is, as much as I love you, I don't want to be like you or Dad. Definitely not like Dad. I want to be my own person. But I don't seem able to escape my fate." I took a giant lick of my ice cream, which was a mistake because it was really cold.

She stopped laughing and wiped her eyes with the utterly pointless, tiny square napkins they give you. I couldn't believe it, but her cone was holding up under the weight of all those marshmallows and nuts. It could come crashing down at any moment, but she was oblivious to the danger.

"Family isn't destiny, Guinevere. That's something I'm learning for myself, but you should know it too. You can forge your own path. And boy, are you forging it."

I took tiny licks of my cone as I considered the extraordinary statement. Mom licked her cone until the dividing line between the two scoops merged into one, then she continued.

"You don't have to be like me. Or your dad. Definitely not like your dad."

I gave her a thumbs up, which she returned.

"You're not like us. And that's good. You're not even like my mom and that's a miracle because you spend so much time with her. You're all Guinevere. Bold, original, and weird in your own way. May as well embrace it, because there's no getting around it."

"But, I'm trying to be normal."

"I'm not sure it's working for you. You're the only fourteen-year-old I've ever heard of who asked for an iron for a back-to-school gift. And the only one who enjoys watching *The Lawrence Welk Show* with her grandparents."

"So? It grows on you."

"Like a fungus."

We both laughed. She was not wrong.

I sighed and started nibbling around the edge of the cone. "I guess I'll never be nice."

"That's ridiculous. You are nice. A mean person wouldn't have stood up for Ronald. A mean person wouldn't have made him Romeo in the first place."

Somehow, I felt that we were working with different definitions of "nice." Language was slippery like that. My definition was more like the middle-class morality Dad mentioned, and hers was more just being a decent person.

"I'm proud of you. It takes courage to stand up to the hateful old biddies in this neighborhood. I never could. I just try to avoid them. Just keep doing your own thing—starched shirt and all."

We sat silently, licking our ice cream as the birds flew south overhead, swirling and circling but ultimately heading in the same direction, except for the random ones that flew in a straight line. But even those straight-shooters were going the same way—they just got there before the others.

I thought about The Call. It was so clear when I heard it and started the whole normalcy project. I wondered if I'd messed up the translation, language being slippery and all. Maybe the problem with me wasn't that God didn't like who I was, but that I didn't, and so heard what I wanted to hear, a command to remake myself before I could be accepted.

I didn't know. All I knew was that I wanted something. Not as narrow as what Charity Louise had, but not as expansive as what my parents had either. They were so flexible in their thinking that they'd try anything that sparkled, until they got bored and went on to the next thing.

I wanted something solid, but welcoming. A little vanilla, but never boring. And as a lover of vanilla, I knew that vanilla was never boring, with variations in flavor from buttery to spicy. It was smooth, easy, and dependable—and it never broke the cone.

Over our heads, the birds massed and swirled.

"Are you really OK with me doing my own thing, or is it just something Moms are supposed to say?"

"I'm truly OK with it. If it doesn't hurt anyone else. And it's legal. And it doesn't involve drugs. Or sex. Or flunking out of school."

"That's a lot of conditions."

"Were you planning to do any of those?"

"No."

"Good. Those are my terms."

"Acceptable."

She narrowed her eyes. "I know that look. Your wheels are spinning. You're planning something."

"No, I was thinking that since I've been to like a hundred churches with you and Dad, I'm qualified to pick my own. Can I?"

"I have no objections."

"Even if it's Mamaw's church?"

She rolled her eyes but kept smiling. "Even if it's Mamaw's church."

We finished our ice cream and headed to the car.

"I can't believe I got sent to the principal's office and ended up with ice cream."

"Make sure it's the last time. That's an order. I don't have time for it. If I make it through this semester, I can finally quit my office job and start earning money as a nurse. But only if I make it through the semester. No more drama."

"I promise."

"I'm going over to Cherry's to hang out tonight. Timmy's been complaining that he never sees you anymore. Want to come?"

"As tempting as that is," I smirked, "tonight is the homecoming dance. If I can find something to wear."

"Oh, yeah. I thought you were making something."

"I didn't finish."

Mom tilted her head, considering. "You know, I'm a pretty good seamstress. I can give Cherry a raincheck. Wouldn't want you to miss meeting up with that cute boy you were talking to in the hall." She winked.

I blushed. "I might, maybe, possibly, have a date."

"What kind of dress is it?"

"Not a dress. It's one of those full prairie skirts and a top with puffy sleeves. You know, like a frilly Little House look, with ribbons. And stupid pintucks."

She looked worried. "You didn't get a Gunne Sax pattern, did you?"

That is exactly what I got. They were notorious for being difficult but were so pretty. I'd done alright with most of the skirt, but the shirt was way above my skill set.

"Yeah, I did."

"Well, we'd better get home. If we hurry, we might just finish in time."

Chapter 19

Hey Fourteen, You Stink!

Working together, Mom and I finished the skirt; she sewed while I kept the cats from climbing up the fabric. My prairie skirt was full and gathered, purple with tiny lavender and brown flowers scattered all over. White eyelet lace flounced at mid-calf. It looked perfect with pantyhose and the black ballerina flats I'd found at TG&Y.

Mom was a great seamstress, but she wasn't a fairy godmother. There was no "Bibbidi-Bobbidi-Boo." She said it was impossible to finish all the pintucks and ribbon trim on the blouse unless I wanted to arrive at the dance after midnight. I wore my white bow blouse instead, the one I usually wore with my favorite red jumper. Mom did my hair in one French braid and curled tendrils of hair in front of my ears. She let me use her smoky eyeshadow.

I couldn't believe it, but I looked great. Watch out, Matt! I was going to knock him out.

Mom drove me to the dance, but as usual, I asked her to park around the corner from the rec center. I don't know why I bothered, though. I'd bet everyone could hear Swooshie from a block away because she was rumbling something fierce. The muffler. Swooshie's had fallen off.

"Pick me up here, too, OK?"

"I can pick you up at the front door."

"No, here is fine."

"You sure it's not too close?"

"Parents! Always with the sarcasm." I swung open the door and put my foot out on the curb, but Mom's voice pulled me back.

"Hey. I'm sorry I've been so distracted lately. I enjoyed your performance. And I'd like to see your halftime show. Maybe I can watch from outside the fence sometime. The biddies! You know what they're like."

I did know what they were like. I blinked, trying to keep the tears that had leapt to my eyes from messing up the smoky eyeshadow. "I understand, Mom. Coach Jamey said you're really brave to be an adult-learning student."

Mom eyes sparkled. I kind of felt like she was suppressing a giggle. "I appreciate that. Tell Coach Jamey, 'Thank you.'"

The PTA moms, led by Mrs. Walters, manned the admission table. I handed over my $2 without a care and walked into the gym with my head held high. I was so over them. Who cared if they thought I was nice or not? I sure didn't.

The gym still smelled like sweaty socks and puberty, but the Student Council had worked a miracle with the decorations. Wendy might not be the nicest person in the world, but she sure could order people to string crepe paper to perfection. It hung from the ceiling and the basketball goals. Everywhere you could hang crepe paper, there it was. And despite what Susan said, it didn't look like toilet paper in the trees. And despite what Jerica said, it didn't look like a party store had barfed. It looked magical and mystical as it swayed in the darkened gym.

I looked for Matt, but the gym floor was a morass of bodies grooving to Hall and Oates. I sang along, "Ooh-ooh ooh-ooh-ooh." Nothing would make my dreams come true like finding Matt for our sorta-kinda-maybe date.

Finally, I glimpsed his blonde hair, and I couldn't believe I hadn't noticed it when I walked into the room. It gleamed in the fractured light of the disco ball. I started walking towards him, but then I caught a glimpse of who he was dancing with and stopped.

Wendy.

She looked smug. Like she deserved everything she got. As usual.

She also looked like a million bucks, wearing a pin-tucked and ribboned, sleeveless Gunne Sax dress that I bet she bought ready-made in a fancy department store at the mall on the other side of the river. I was surprised she wasn't dancing with Ronnie because everyone knew their future marriage was written in the stars.

I was trying to decide whether I should interrupt them, because Mike had said he'd see me tonight, when I was tackled by Denise.

"You look amazing!" she gushed.

"No, you look amazing!" Her hair was perfectly feathered, and her peasant-style blouse was adorable—and strangely filled out around the chest. "Denise! Your bust exercises worked," I whispered.

"I..." Her words were drowned out by giggling and the thump of the bass.

"You what?"

She was wearing heels, and I was wearing flats, so for the first time, she didn't have to stand on tiptoe to reach my ear. "Stuffed. I stuffed my bra." Her eyes sparkled mischievously.

"Your secret is safe with me. You look amazing."

"Face it, I look the most amazing!" Susan flicked her long, straight hair.

"Va-va-voom!" She did, in fact, look the most amazing in her one-shoulder, shiny, red dress. She looked like a woman. Denise and I looked like little girls. "Where did you get that dress?"

"My aunt's closet. She bought it a few years ago during her Disco phase."

Suddenly, the lights went out completely. We shrieked. Then the strobe light pulsed, and we squealed at the familiar rhythm of the drum and the thump of the bass, "ba-ba-ba-ba-BAH Bah Bah," thundering from the DJ's hi-fi. We screamed in unison, "Whip it!"

Holding hands, we rushed the dance floor, pogoing like maniacs and singing our heads off. I forgot all about Matt.

I was crazy sweaty by the time the song ended, so we headed out of the gym to cool off. I spotted Matt in a big group of the usual crowd, standing under a crepe-paper draped basketball goal.

"Wait up," I said to Susan and Denise. "I'm going to say 'Hi' to Matt."

They took my arms and pulled me away, into the light, where I blinked and got in the concession stand line to buy a can of pop.

"Didn't you hear?" Denise whispered and looked over her shoulder at Mrs. Walters.

"What?"

"About Wendy and Matt?"

My heart dropped into my stomach, but my brain pushed back. It was impossible. Only hours ago, Matt had said he'd see me at the dance. That set an expectation. It meant he'd at least ask me to dance. This was one of those things, like Rhonda and Brandon doing it in the graveyard: a mean and totally untrue rumor.

"What about them?" I asked, pushing the tab on the pop can back and forth until it broke off.

"They're going with each other."

"Since when?" I asked, trying to keep the choking sound out of my voice.

Susan rubbed my back. It made me think that they'd guessed my crush as easily as Ronald had. Boy, was I a lousy actress.

"Sometime this afternoon, I guess," said Denise.

"Wendy-schmindy," said Susan. "Let's Dance."

I did my best to have fun, but my heart wasn't in it 100%. Eventually, I told them I was going to sit out a few dances. So, they joined Jerica and Rhonda on the dance floor. Charity Louise wasn't there because she thought dancing was sinful. And Tonya wasn't there because her boyfriend was an adult, and the dance committee wouldn't let him in. Ronald stayed home watching TV to give everyone a chance to forget about our kiss. I think he was still afraid of being lynched, which made me feel terrible that I'd agreed to let be in the talent show with me in the first place. I stood against the wall and watched.

The opening notes of "Endless Love" started playing while the disco ball rotated slowly, casting its fragmented light across the room. I watched as Wendy grabbed Matt's hand and pulled him away from the group of football players he was talking to and onto the dance floor. It made me wish Ronald were there, standing against the wall with me. I felt like he would have understood what I was feeling.

Ronnie Mills, glaring after them, took the hand of the nearest girl, a very surprised Denise.

Susan ran a few steps towards me, emphatically pointing and mouthing, *Look, look!*

While I watched the drama unfold, I was caught off guard. I didn't notice Michael Michael's inch up beside me, and that was saying something, because he was like six feet tall. He cleared his throat a couple of times while Lionel Ritchie and Diana Ross sang about two hearts beating as one. I tried to pretend he wasn't there, and then I felt bad because I didn't want to hurt his feelings; I just didn't want to dance with him. And then I made the mistake of looking sideways at him and smiling just a little, and that's when he got brave enough to say what we all knew he was waiting to say.

"Do-ya-wanna-dance?" He burst out, asking the question as one word and following it up with a swallow.

I took a breath. Could I say no? I didn't think so. It seemed so mean here in the gym with eyes on us, even though most of those eyes were following the Wendy-Matt-Ronnie-Denise Spectacle. I was worried someone might notice the Marcus-Guinevere-Tragedy of Awkwardness unfolding. And even though my Ways to Be Normal list was crumbling, the one thing I held firm to was, "Don't Be a Jerk."

"Sure," I said.

On the dance floor, I put my hands on Michael's shoulders and locked my elbows. His hands on my waist were sweaty. I guessed he was nervous. He said something, but I didn't hear the words because I was watching Wendy and Matt around his shoulder.

"What?" I asked, relaxing my elbows and leaning forward a smidge.

"It's a nice song," he said again.

"Yeah, it is."

We swayed. It was embarrassing. I couldn't think of anything to say. I saw Wendy slip her hands behind Matt's neck. I realized Michael had spoken again.

"What?" I asked.

"Did you see the movie?"

"Which one?"

"*Endless Love*. You know? The song."

"Oh, of course. Yeah. I saw it."

"Romantic," he said.

I raised both eyebrows. "In a completely obsessive, unhealthy way. Sure. Romantic."

He seemed confused. Luckily, he stopped talking. I went back to watching Wendy and Matt as she angled her head onto his shoulder. When she finally made it there, some of her hairspray-coated hair got into his mouth. He made such a funny face that I laughed.

"Gesundheit!" said Michael.

"What?" I asked.

"You sneezed."

I smiled. No need to tell him he was wrong. "Thank you."

The final Ooo-ooo-ooo's of the song ended, and we went our separate ways. Michael didn't look back. I'm pretty sure he was relieved it was over. I knew I was.

I looked for Denise to ask how her dance with Ronnie went, but then the DJ started playing "Open Arms." Two slow dances in a row were too much. I decided to leave the dance and hang out with Molly until it was time for Mom to pick me up.

I had left the gym and was just about to push the exit bar to leave the rec center when I heard my name.

"Martha?"

Dammit! Why was he the only one who remembered my name? I turned and there he was, shining, even in the cruddy fluorescent lights of the rec center. "Hey, Matt."

"Leaving?"

"Obviously. You and Wendy?"

"Yeah. Obviously, I guess." It was weird, but he didn't sound happy about it.

"When did you ask her?"

"Umm. Didn't really."

"Did she ask you?"

"Not exactly. It was kind of...well...her mom."

I couldn't help it. A laugh burst out of me. "You're kidding?"

He laughed too. "Yeah. If it gets out, my cool guy image will be blown."

"What cool guy image?"

"Good point."

"Do you like her?" I held my breath, waiting.

"She's OK."

I had been hoping for a straight-up, "no." Guess I'd have to live with disappointment.

"You should probably go back to the gym. Her mom's probably looking for you."

"Yeah, you're probably right."

I turned to push the exit bar on the door, but he stopped me.

"Martha? You're not walking home, are you?"

"No, my mom's coming."

"Good. I'm glad."

And with a lingering glance, he walked back into the gym.

I sat on Molly's grave and cried.

Why wasn't I good enough?

Not nice.

Not normal.

Not now.

Not ever.

Chapter 20

We All Need Help to Feel Fine

"Plans for tonight?"

"None. I'm going to lie on this bed and stare at Scott Baio. Maybe watch TV."

"No offense to Chachi, but that sounds like a miserable evening."

"So, the usual."

I didn't tell Mom what happened at the dance, because I didn't want to talk about it, but when she picked me up at the corner and saw my tear-streaked mascara and smudged smoky eye shadow, she immediately knew it wasn't great.

"Why don't you come with me? Cherry hasn't seen you in ages. She misses your 'sparkling sense of humor.' A direct quote, I might add. She told me when I had lunch with her last week."

Cherry was cool. And she thought I was cool. She didn't have to think that. She could have been distant but polite, like I was with Timmy, who was the antithesis of cool. Plus, she was smart. Maybe not smarter than my mom, but she noticed things that Mom couldn't see. For instance, several years ago, she was the one who told my mom that I needed to start wearing a training bra. Maybe I'd go, just to make Cherry happy. Since she missed me and all. Not because I needed company or wisdom or anything. I rolled off the bed.

"OK. Where are we going?" By which I meant, what should I wear?

I settled on a pale blue button-down Oxford shirt (Pinpoint cotton, starched and ironed, thank you very much!) and jeans with a ribbon belt. Casual, but neat enough to let the slobs know I wasn't one of them.

Thanks to Gerald replacing the muffler, Swooshie drove quietly across the river to the other side of town, where I saw the familiar blue and yellow head shop in the distance. Honestly, Mom wasn't into grass. She was responsible, even if she didn't want to be, probably because of me. But her friends were into it, except, ironically, her best friend, Cherry, who worked at the shop. I swear it is not exaggerating to say that most of my formative years had been frittered away sitting in the back room waiting for

Cherry to get off work. Hours I'd never get back. The only good thing about hanging out there, other than getting to see Cherry, is that I knew I'd never smoke pot. It smelled disgusting and it made you act like an idiot. It wasn't for me.

The night started as boring as usual, and to make it even better—that's sarcasm, if you didn't know—Timmy was there.

As soon as I walked through the door, he came bounding over.

"Hi, Guinevere."

"It's Martha. Remember? I told my mom to tell your mom."

"Oh yeah. She told me. It's just you've been Guinevere my whole life. It's hard to change."

His eyes flickered to my chest, and he became dumb. Well, dumber. He'd never had a lot going on upstairs.

While he stammered, my mom's friend Daryl came over and put his hand on my shoulder. He whistled, low and skeezy.

"Well, well, little girl, haven't you grown?" His eyes swept up and down, then settled on my boobs. "You look NICE! Your mom's gonna have to lock you away. Hey, Fawn, you're gonna have to lock this girl up or she'll be all kiiiinds of trouble." He whistled again.

What with coming to the talent show and helping me with my outfit for the dance and all, Mom had been acting like a normal Mom. But now? She laughed! While her skeezeball friend tried to undress me with his eyes! She was too busy flirting with some sappy dope to notice I was practically being molested under her nose. Geesh, and all for a sap that could quote Kahlil Gibran but couldn't hold down a job. According to Mamaw, that was the only kind of guy Mom liked.

Timmy was no help. While I broke out in a cold sweat, he giggled like a girl. It was a nervous giggle. Very nervous, like he was as freaked out about Daryl as I was, but still—he did nothing.

Thank God for Cherry.

She noticed my dilemma and offered a way out.

"Martha, come help me with these boxes."

Another great thing about her, she remembered my name.

I hurried over to where she was unpacking merchandise to display on the store shelves. Timmy followed me.

"Scoot, I want to talk to Martha."

One more thing to love about her.

"But—"

"Vamoose."

He stomped away and crashed on a bean bag.

Cherry shook her head. "That kid! Did you know, boys mature more slowly than girls?"

"Ha. I didn't, but it doesn't surprise me. Boys are dipsticks. I'm swearing them off."

"Sounds serious. Any boy in particular?"

I shrugged, evading the question. "Maybe."

"Is that why you changed your name?"

"No, the name change happened before I decided to cut boys out of my life."

"Tell me about it."

"You sure? It might take a while."

"I've got all night. You talk. I'll unpack these decorative doodads."

I squinted at the wonky statuette she held. "What is that, anyway?"

"I'm not sure. People buy weird junk when they're high."

So, I sat on a poof and told her the whole sad story, top to bottom. "And finally, I figured if I was going to have any chance of becoming normal, I needed to change my name. Because nobody's name is Guinevere. In the real world, anyway."

Cherry chuckled and sat on a stepstool. "I understand about your name, even though I think it's beautiful. The boys used to tease me about my name. All of it sexual. Can you imagine?"

"Oof. I can. That was rude."

"It was so embarrassing." She put her elbows on her knees and leaned towards me. "Where I get lost in your story, Martha, is the whole abandoning who you are because God spoke to you from a Pontiac while a Hammond organ played in the background and a cheerleading jacket flashed before your eyes thing."

I scrunched my face. "Yeah, it does sound kind of kooky when you put it like that."

"Just a little." She laughed, then got serious again. "But here's the thing, I'm no expert, but I've been reading my Bible lately, trying to turn my life around—but you don't need to know all that. Anyway, there's this Psalm I keep reading: 'For you created my inmost being; you knit me together in my mother's womb. I praise you because I am fearfully and wonderfully made; your works are wonderful, I know that full well.'"

"That's beautiful. Which Psalm is it? I need to look it up."

"139. And it is beautiful. You're beautiful. And wonderful. It says so right there in the Bible. God made you, and me, individually. We didn't come off a mass-market production line like those doodads on the shelf. That blows my mind. He wants us to follow him, and live our lives according to scripture, but I just can't believe he wants you to hide the unique person he made you to be whatever version of "normal" you've decided you need to be."

"You've been talking to my mom."

"You know, we've talked pretty much every day since the day we met in kindergarten."

"I do believe I've heard that story."

She laughed and stood up so she could put the stepstool away. "I'll be the first to admit that I'm still working things out for myself. But think about what I said, alright?"

"I will. I promise."

"Oh, by the way, there's a book in my bag I think you'll like. I just finished it. Sit back here and read and I'll make them stay clear." She pointed at the chest-oglers.

"I love you!" I wrapped my arms around her.

"And me, you, Martha."

I found her bag and took out the thick book, weighing it in my hands. It was heavy. If I didn't like the story, I could use it as a weapon if Daryl came slinking around. I turned to the last page and whispered, "Yes!" There were 972 pages. The worst thing in the world, other than skeezeballs, was finishing a book in a single afternoon when you wanted the story to go on forever. And lately, I'd been reading so many teen romances that they never lasted longer than a day. Cherry's book would keep me busy for a long time.

I turned the old green book over and looked at the spine. The title was stamped in faded gold:

Forever
Amber

~

Kathleen
Winsor

That was it. There was no synopsis on the back. No recommendations from famous authors. No picture on the cover. Nothing to preview the excitement within.

I sat cross-legged behind the shelf and opened the book to the first chapter, "1644."

I began to read.

It wasn't long before Timmy, Skeezy Daryl, Mom, the sappy guy, and the funky smell of the head shop faded away. When closing time came and we moved across the street to get coneys, I kept reading, interrupted only briefly by Timmy.

"Guinevere, how many coneys are you getting?"

I glared at him over the top of the open book.

"I mean, Martha..."

His voice trailed off as I lowered my eyes and kept reading.

By page twenty-four, when Amber St. Clare raised her arm, pointed, and uttered her first, "M'lord," I was hooked. And by page forty-five, when Amber and Lord Carlton DID IT for the first time, I was obsessed.

I can't remember what else happened that night except that once we finally went home, Cherry let me keep the book.

Chapter 21

Against the Wind, and the Grain

I THOUGHT ABOUT WHAT Cherry said. And then I walked over to Mamaw's church for Sunday service and thought about it more. I even thought about it a little while eating pot roast and pineapple upside-down cake with her and Gerald after church. But mainly I read.

When Monday morning rolled around, I was still reading. I read while I ate generically frosted corn flakes and milk, and I read while walking down The Hill. At school, I reluctantly exchanged *Forever Amber* for my textbooks. But when library period came around, I sprang it from my locker, which smelled like the corn chips of generations past even though I'd put a couple of the scented, shell-shaped soaps from Mamaw's bathroom inside to freshen it up.

I took my assigned seat in the library and propped the enormous volume open on the table. My tablemates exchanged looks. I could guess what they were thinking. Weirdo. Show-off. Nerd. I knew they'd never read a book with so many pages, especially not that spaz, Stacy Nelson. But for once, I didn't care about being weird. Amber's story was too exciting to be distracted by questions of normality.

I was on page 654. Fire was destroying London. Amber was desperately trying to get to the bank to save her money. I had to find out what happened next because I had biology after library period. I'd never be able to concentrate on cellular structure when I had The Great Fire on my brain.

The librarian, Miss Thompson, was a short, squat old biddy with steel gray curls and sensible shoes. She was about 107, and I was sure she'd been wearing the same two tweed skirt suits all those years. She was the kind of librarian who assigned career reports the first day of school every year. For three years running, I'd told her I wanted to be an actress, and for three years running, she'd replied that it was impractical. She made me do reports about being a secretary instead, which I'll admit is a very normal thing to be, but maybe a little too normal, especially after Coach Jamey put thoughts of college in my head. Anyway, you can see what Miss Thompson was like.

With my head in 17th-century London, I didn't pay attention to the creak of her sensible shoes as she circled our table until she stopped opposite me.

Gasp!

I looked up to see her tight little curls quivering in indignation.

She hissed, "Guinevere MacKenzie, come with me this instant. And bring that book!"

And then she did the unthinkable; a sure sign of impending Armageddon: she left the library with students still in it. I was so shocked, I didn't even tell her to call me Martha.

The collected eyes of my twenty-six classmates swiveled in my direction. That was fifty-two eyeballs searing into me, Guinevere, who wanted to be Martha and not, under any circumstances, stick out in a crowd.

I dog-eared page 656 to mark my place and slid out of my chair. I started to slump out under the gaze of those fifty-two eyeballs, a practice I'd developed to hide my generous bust development, but then I got mad. I knew I'd done nothing wrong. So, I threw back my shoulders, dangerously straining the buttons of my green, above-the-knee shirtdress across the chest as I marched into the hall to be chewed out by the librarian. Somebody whistled, and I'd swear someone else said "what a babe" before I got out the door.

Curls bristling, Miss Thompson pointed to the principal's office across the hall.

My fourth trip to the office and the first quarter wasn't over; once every 10.2 days. At the rate I was going, I'd have a reserved seat by Christmas.

I hugged the book to my chest and looked at the ceiling. If it had split apart to welcome the Second Coming, I wouldn't have minded even though I'd still never kissed a boy. I didn't count Ronald because that was just acting.

Principal Duncan leaned on the counter, talking to the secretaries and Mrs. Walters, who stood at her usual place by the mimeograph machine. He stubbed out his cigarette when Miss Thompson staggered in, sputtering, "Must see you! At once! Very serious!"

Geesh, she was so upset she couldn't speak in complete sentences, but I still didn't know what I'd done.

Mrs. Walters' eyes sparkled with interest and glee. This was why she volunteered in the office.

The chair in front of Mr. Duncan's desk squeaked when I sat, and I knew my nervous sweat would cause the backs of my thighs to stick to the orange vinyl. I thumbed the pages of the heavy tome I held in my lap, which seemed to be the cause of this visit to the principal's lair, though I couldn't think why. Uncertainty hung so heavily in the air that it almost crowded out the cigarette smoke.

One of the secretaries briskly handed Mr. Duncan a file, then sauntered out, taking time to give me the side-eye. The other secretary and Mrs. Walters lurked near the door. They were as interested in finding out what I'd done as I was. I didn't have to wait long because Miss Thompson started right in.

"Mr. Duncan, this student has brought a book of...of smut. A smutty book. She's brought a book about...sex...to school. And she was reading it in the library."

Gasps came from the outer office.

The principal's eyebrows raised slightly, but otherwise, he looked bored.

I couldn't believe it! She'd sent me to the office for a dirty book?! There was an entire shelf of Judy Blume books in the library. Why did she think we checked them out? The warm life lessons? It was a complete injustice. I sat up straighter and raised my chin.

Mr. Duncan flipped open my file and scanned it. "After two years of peace, I've seen a lot of you lately, Guinevere."

"Don't I know it, sir. And if you don't mind, it's Martha."

His responding look contained a question.

"My name, sir, it's Martha."

"You're saying I have the wrong file. That there's another Miss MacKenzie in this school."

"No, sir, I'm saying I changed my name. A couple of weeks ago."

Mr. Duncan rubbed a spot between his eyebrows.

Miss Thompson tutted as if my name change was a sure sign of my downward spiral—and we all knew where it would end. "Mr. Duncan, what are you going to do about that book and this girl?"

"But Miss Thompson," I said, "it's not inappropriate. It's educational. I mean, did you know there was a terrible plague in England? And that London burned down? Well, I didn't until I read this book."

"It was banned, Miss MacKenzie."

"Banned? When?"

"In 1946."

After a heavy pause, Mr. Duncan spoke up, "Times have changed, Miss Thompson."

"Good morals never change, Mr. Duncan."

He looked at the pack of cigarettes on his desk like Lord Carlton first looked at the valley of Amber's breasts. Then he sighed and closed the file with a slap. "This is what we'll do. I'll hang onto the book and call your mother. If she wants you to have the book, she can come to the office to get it."

"But—"

"No buts."

Was it only last week that I'd promised Mom I'd keep things on an even keel? She would never take off to come get my book. She'd say it served me right for taking it to school in the first place, and she'd ground me just because she could. I'd never find out what happened with that fire.

I left the office mad, and the more I thought about it, the madder I got. It didn't help that everyone was talking about "Crazy Guinevere and her trip to the principal's office" either. They all seemed to know why, though most people got it wrong and said I'd brought a sex manual to school. Tonya asked if she could take a peek at it if I ever got it back.

My entire life plan of trying to be normal was well and truly busted. Nothing I'd tried had worked. And after talking to Cherry, I was pretty sure that I'd misunderstood God's plan for me. I still believed he wanted good things for me, but I was going about it the wrong way. With that being the case, why shouldn't I go whole hog and come up with a plan to get my book back? Without my mom knowing about it.

The first step was to make sure Mom didn't get the call. That semester, she'd been getting home from work at about the same time I got home from school before going to her night shift at the hospital. So, instead of going to Denise's house like I'd planned, I ran straight home after school, took the phone off the hook, and hid the receiver under my pillow so Mom wouldn't hear the off-the-hook beeping. At 4:01, I stealthily put the phone back where it belonged. Susan's cousin Bobby, who's in the principal's office about twice a week, told me that Mr. Duncan never calls after four because he has to get home to give his wife a break from their juvenile delinquent kids. Mom never noticed a thing.

I spent the rest of the evening hidden away in my bedroom, working on step two: posters. I couldn't believe it, but I was taking a page from my mom and dad's playbook. Neither of them was exactly parent of the year material, but they used to stand for something, even though it was weird hippie stuff. They took me to some marches when I was a baby, but I couldn't remember anything about them. I asked Dad once why he dropped it all, and he said he got burned out and disillusioned. It's why he tried out so many churches and relationships, I guessed, looking for something to stand for.

The next morning, I put step three into action. Instead of going to class, I set up in the hall across from the office. I taped three big posters on the wall that said, "Sit-In to End Oppression," and "Say No to Censorship," and "Books Aren't Dangerous." I sat cross-legged on the floor in front of them.

It was not a Martha kind of thing to do, but I didn't care.

Right off the bat, a couple of kids joined me. They were mainly the kids who always skipped class anyway, but I appreciated the company.

I sat there all morning. Eventually, the other kids got bored and wandered back to class or over to the Stop-n-Go to smoke. I could see Mr. Duncan in the office rubbing that spot on his forehead and talking to the secretaries. I overheard snatches of their conversations.

"Called. Mom's not home. No answering machine."

"...constitutional rights."

"She'll get bored."

"...skimmed the book...not that bad...but Thompson..."

At lunchtime, I tried to get Susan and Denise to sit with me.

Susan rolled her eyes and said, "Fat chance...Martha."

Denise said that if it were any other day, she'd do it, but it was bean chowder and cinnamon roll day in the cafeteria, and she wasn't going to miss out.

Some friends!

Matt sat with me for a little while. He gave me half of his bologna sandwich. Foxy and nice; one in a million. Too bad I didn't have a chance since he was going with Wendy and all. But? If he was going with Wendy, why was he sitting with me? I had to know.

"Did you have fun at the dance?"

"Not really." He stuck out his tongue, maybe remembering the taste of Wendy's hairspray.

"But you and Wendy? You're a thing, right?"

"Nope. That was a mistake."

When he smiled, I was reminded how much I loved the way his front tooth crossed a little over the one beside it.

He said the whole school was talking about me. They thought it was cool that I was sticking it to the man, and everyone, except for Charity Louise, thought it was unfair of the principal to take my sex manual. He said that even Wendy thought it was cool, and if I ever got my book back, she wanted to see it.

I never thought I wanted to stand out, but I could get used to being a celebrity. Weird, I know, but I figured if

Miss Thompson and Mrs. Walters were representatives of the normal, I'd take a pass.

When my English teacher, Mrs. Greenberg, came clomping down the hall in her clogs, I figured she was going to tell me off for missing her class, but all she did was point to Matt and say, "Back to class, Madewell," before going into the office. When she came out, she was carrying my book. She held it out to me.

I cradled it in my arms. "How did you get it?"

"I simply told Mr. Duncan that you're the only student in this school willing to read a thousand-page book and that suppressing exceptional intelligence is an appalling thing for an educator to do. He agreed. And honestly, I think he just wanted to be done with the whole thing."

"Exceptional?"

"Yes. Exceptional. But don't let it go to your head. Come to class."

My smile was about to split my face in two when I turned to take the posters from the wall.

"No, don't. Leave them," she said, "but do me one favor, Martha, don't bring that book back to school. If you do, Miss Thompson will probably have a heart attack and we don't want that on our hands, now do we?" She winked.

"I won't, Mrs. Greenberg, and...you can call me Guinevere."

Martha was normal, but Guinevere was not only exceptional, she was wonderful, it said so right in the Bible. And if she was good enough for God, Cherry, and Mrs. Greenberg, she was good enough for me.

Chapter 22
Call Me Guinevere

"Can I take your plate?"

The sweet, young tones of the waiter, evocative of the hopeful and anxious voices that filled my reverie, brought me back to the present.

"Of course, thank you."

I smile at the handsome young man, blonde and fit like another young man I knew well, and pray he has friends like mine; friends to buoy him through the hard times.

"Want another, G?" Susan asks, lifting her empty wine glass to make her meaning clear.

"Oh, no. Don't give her another. She hasn't said a word in twenty minutes, and that's a straight-up miracle."

I laugh. "You're right, Charity. I do believe I've had enough."

"It's because we're so damn old," says Rhonda, "our tolerance has decreased."

"Wait, I thought we were calling ourselves middle-aged." Denise giggles. She's definitely had enough.

"Girl, middle age is in the rearview mirror, and I have the AARP card to prove it," says Jerica.

"And the gray." Susan flicks her hair, still long and straight, but the black shimmers with streaks of silver.

The breeze on the restaurant's deck overlooking the lake blows the mist from my thoughts, but a few backward-looking strands hold tight, stirring in the current like crepe paper streamers hung from a basketball goal. And as I look at the rippling moonlight splashed over the water, I'm reminded of what the famous poet mused, that all time is eternally here, in this moment, the present and the past, mingled with the future. I can't help thinking that the door I left closed, the "What might have been," didn't lead to a rose garden, but to thorns. And it's all because of that pivotal year, and these friends, and others too.

I am better for it.

"The night is young, let's sit on the dock."

"But it's way down there. So many stairs."

"Are you middle-aged or old, Denise?"

"Not old. I'm coming. But why stairs?"

"What about you, Guinevere? Coming? Or are you calling lover boy?"

I close my eyes, and the breeze stirs my hair and my thoughts. "No, he's out with the boys. But give me a minute, I want to enjoy the view."

There's one more memory to relive.

MY CELEBRITY STATUS LASTED the rest of the day, even after people took a look at my sex manual and discovered it was no such thing.

Wendy was disappointed once she got ahold of it.

"Leave it to my mom to get it totally wrong," she said, shaking her head.

Confirmation of how the rumor had gotten started in the first place.

"Oh, well. It takes balls to do what you did." She handed the book back to me. "Friends?"

"Sure." I figured it was more like a truce. True friendship required trust, and I didn't trust Wendy anymore. It was hard to believe I ever had.

I was high-fived for sticking it to the administration so many times on my way to my locker that by the time I got there, the halls were almost empty.

Enter Matt, stage right, peeking mischievously around the edge of my open locker door.

"Boo!"

"Eek!" I threw my hands up in fake surprise. "What's up, you wascally wabbit?"

"I was going to ask you the same thing."

"Not much. I told my grandma I'd help her in her print shop tonight, but that's about it."

"I have football practice later, but I can walk with you part of the way. If you want."

Be still, my fluttering heart. No way was I turning him down.

"Sure, that would be fine," I said, trying not to sound too eager.

We took the long way, out the front door, past the rec center, and through the winding streets of the neighborhood. It was still warm, but there was a nip on the breeze that let you know fall had arrived. The leaves on the trees that curved over the asphalt-paved streets were edged with orange and red, and yellow.

In all of the teen romances I'd read lately, the boy and the girl smile shyly at each other and don't know what to say, but there was none of that with Matt. I told him the details of getting sent to the office, including Miss Thompson's quivering curls and Mr. Duncan's longing looks at his cigarettes, and Matt laughed lustily, like I imagined Lord Carlton laughed with Amber, in all the right places.

"Oh, look. The cemetery. Come on, I want you to meet someone."

He smiled and shook his head, as I'd seen him do dozens of times, like I was the weirdest person he'd ever met, but he liked it. "OK, Martha, I'm up for a scare."

"Oh, I forgot to tell you. I've given up on Martha. You can call me Guinevere, if you don't mind."

"I don't. It suits you." And he nodded like that wasn't a bad thing at all.

I introduced him to Molly, and we sat, talking about the day and the week and the year and all the years before. Of clarinet and part-time jobs and shows on television. We talked until the sounds of football practice echoed across the field and over the cemetery fence, but Matt didn't move.

Except to lean closer to me.

He smelled like fall leaves and Old Spice cologne, and that stuff Mamaw rubbed on her muscles when they ached. He smelled good.

And I knew what was happening. I was finally going to have my first real kiss. The first one that mattered.

He inched closer. I was on the cusp. The kiss of all kisses; the one I'd remember when I was old and gray. But after all the buildup, I wasn't sure I was ready. Was it because I'd just started figuring out who I was and didn't want to get distracted, or because I was scared? I didn't know, probably a little of both, but I went with my instincts.

"Look, a ghost," I said.

"Where?" Matt's head whipped around.

"There, by the fence."

He pulled his feet up like he was ready to bolt if a ghost appeared.

And then a toad emerged from the bushes. It croaked.

Matt laughed. "That toad sounds like you playing the clarinet." He put his hands behind his head and leaned back on Mr. Thomas Perry Parmley's gravestone. Smiling, he stared through the leaves at the faded blue sky. "You're right, Guinevere. It's nice here."

I leaned back against Molly and gazed at the same sky Matt was looking at, hugging my good feelings to myself.

One of these days, I'd kiss Matt Madewell, but not now. Not yet.

For now, loving Guinevere was enough.

What's True and What's Not? Plus, Acknowledgements

Guinevere MacKenzie is Not a Nice Girl is a work of fiction.

Guinevere is not me, but I did glean inspiration from many of the events and circumstances of my childhood and mash them together to create Guinevere's story. For instance, my mom's best friend did work in a head shop in which I spent childhood hours hanging out in the backroom. Between my parents and grandparents, I visited a vast variety of religious denominations. And I really did end up picking my own church when I was a teen. Also true, I was on pom squad the first year it was offered in my community, my mom drove a used *Starsky and Hutch* car that I found embarrassing, and I performed the balcony scene on a ladder, but alas, there was no Ronald. Also, the librarian did make me write a report about being a secretary instead of an actress and she scolded me for reading *Forever Amber* by Kathleen Winsor at school and confiscated my book, but I didn't stage a sit-in; I would never have been so bold.

By the way, I reread Amber's story as an adult and it's every bit as exciting as I remembered it to be. If you like historical fiction, I highly recommend it.

My parents divorced when I was a toddler and I grew up in a chaotic home, but Guinevere's parents are not my parents. My thrice-married dad worked as a bartender and was a confirmed Anglophile, but he wasn't gay. My animal-loving, brilliant mom, after dropping out of high school to have me, did get her GED, go to junior college, and build a career as a Respiratory Therapist. It took bravery and effort to juggle it all. I was, and am, proud of her for doing it.

Guinevere's friends and classmates are entirely fictional. I value the friends and enemies I made in middle and high school because they each, in their own way, helped to shape my knowledge of the world, but I did not recreate them here.

However, all the best parts of my grandparents—and there are so many good parts—are represented in Guinevere's grandparents. Which brings me to...

Acknowledgments

Thank you to:

each of my grandparents. As a child & teen, the house I lived in, the vacations I went on, the occasional extracurricular classes I took, were because of them. One grandma taught me to make cookies, paint walls, and develop film in her darkroom. Another grandma took me to my first touring Broadway musical (*A Chorus Line*) and taught me the lyrics to "Que Sera, Sera." Without them, I didn't stand a chance.

my mom, who loved my kids and me fiercely.

my dad, who could charm the socks off a selfish kitten.

my marvelous friend Gaye Sanders who read a draft of this manuscript and loved it. The encouragement meant a lot to me because after working together for five years as leaders of SCBWI OK/AR, I know she knows books.

the Tulsa City-County Library. This novel began life as a short story titled "Call Me Martha," and won the library's annual adult writing contest one year. It was the first writing award I ever won, and it gave me hope that writing was a possibility for me.

my son, Ethan, who came to the awards ceremony when I won the TCCL contest and laughed his head off when I read my story aloud to the audience. He's a tough critic so his unbridled appreciation of my comic writing was the encouragement I needed.

my 8th grade typing teacher at Clinton Middle School in Tulsa, OK. Typing is a useful skill. I'm an exceptional typist. And it's all down to that teacher. It served me well as an administrative assistant (yes, I worked as a secretary), and it serves me better as a writer.

my amazing cover designer, Karina Granda. She designed the cover for my book *A Story Unwritten* as well, and though the two covers are different, they have the same amount of PIZZAZZ! She's talented, kind, and she listens.

my amazingly talented daughters, my hard-working sons-in-law, and my adorable grandkids for making life joyful.

and always, to my husband Kelly for being my partner in all things for 39 years (and counting).

JENNIFER SNEED is a former elementary school teacher and legal assistant. Her articles and short stories have been published in magazines, and she's won a few awards for her writing. She is a leader of the SCBWI OK/AR region. Her debut novel, *A Story Unwritten,* was called "a captivating fairytale adaptation," by Kirkus Reviews. Visit her at www.jennifersneed.com

Thank you for reading this book. Please consider leaving an honest review on Amazon or any other review site. Reviews can be stars-only, one-word, or paragraphs long. You can write a review on any site even if you didn't buy it there. Reviews help writers!